HOLY RULE

We gratefully acknowledge the support of the Canada Council for the Arts and the Ontario Arts Council for our publishing program. We also acknowledge the financial support of the Government of Canada.

Cover design: Val Fullard

Library and Archives Canada Cataloguing in Publication

Coady, Mary Frances, author
        Holy rule / Mary Frances Coady.

(Inanna poetry and fiction series)
Issued in print and electronic formats.
ISBN 978-1-77133-321-4 (paperback). -- ISBN 978-1-77133-322-1 (epub). -- ISBN 978-1-77133-323-8 (kindle). -- ISBN 978-1-77133-324-5 (pdf)

        I. Title. II. Series: Inanna poetry and fiction series

PS8555.O232H65 2016   C813'.54   C2016-904863-2
                                                C2016-904864-0

Printed and bound in Canada

Inanna Publications and Education Inc.
210 Founders College, York University
4700 Keele Street, Toronto, Ontario, Canada M3J 1P3
Telephone: (416) 736-5356 Fax: (416) 736-5765
Email: inanna.publications@inanna.ca Website: www.inanna.ca

MIX
Paper from
responsible sources
FSC
www.fsc.org FSC® C004071

HOLY RULE

a novel by

Mary Frances Coady

inanna poetry & fiction series

INANNA PUBLICATIONS AND EDUCATION INC.
TORONTO, CANADA

For Sharon Goodier

Contents

1. The Interior Castle

THE CONVENT'S LIBRARY DOORKNOB TURNED with a soft click. Lizzie, who had been sitting at the table with a book in front of her and a cigarette butt between two gnarled fingers, turned around to the Boston fern and stubbed the butt into the dirt. Inside the doorway, Sister Antonetta stood looking at her over the tops of round black-rimmed eyeglasses, her lips pursed.

"Having me morning fag just at the minute, Sister," Lizzie said. She rose and smoothed the skirt of her housemaid's dress. "I know I'm to go downstairs, but..." She rubbed the small of her back and fumbled for her cloth duster.

The nun leaned forward, straining to look at a book that sat on the table. Her eyes were small and sharp, her eyebrows flecked with grey. Her black veil fell to just past her shoulders. "What's that?"

"A book, Sister." Lizzie held up the volume to show Sister Antonetta. The title was *The Interior Castle*. The front cover showed a fortress castle with a turret and a high stone wall. "Not a storybook, like I thought, but a nice book all the same." She squinted at the cover. "Saint Teresa of ... of A...," she read aloud. "That's the person that wrote the book. A saint she was." She handed the book to Sister Antonetta. "I'll be getting on with me work, then, Sister."

Lizzie swept the duster over the table, lifting the embroidered cutwork runner that stretched along the top. She paused a moment, gazing at the cloth, and ran a cracked thumbnail along the delicate edging.

Sister Antonetta returned the book to the table and turned to the bookcase across the room. "Crooked as always," she said, reaching up to straighten the calendar on top of the case. The picture on the calendar showed a natural scene full of autumn colour and underneath, in thick black letters, it read "October 1958." Lizzie looked up as, with a soft shuffle, Sister Antonetta removed a handful of books from the middle shelf of the bookcase. She put them on the table beside *The Interior Castle*. Then the nun reached into the back and brought out a plate with a piece of bread on it. The bread had been spread with butter as thick as icing on a cake. She turned to Lizzie.

"For my health," she said. "But *she* won't let me have it. So I take matters into my own hands." She put the plate on the table, picked up the books, and returned them to the shelf. "I have to put it here, so she won't see it." Her thin lips barely moved. Her pale face seemed to blend into the white of the wimple and bandeau framing it.

Lizzie stared at her. "That's a shame, Sister, I'm sure," she said, and resumed her dusting. A piece of fluff was stuck between the table leg and the floor, and she placed her body weight against the leg, lifted it and edged the piece out. Sister Antonetta let out a shriek as the table tipped and both the book and the plate slid off. The bread flopped over, the buttered side clinging to the floor, and the plate lay in three pieces.

"Look what you've done!" Sister Antonetta's face was a mottled pinkish-purple. "My bread and butter!" Her voice rose. "You clumsy woman!"

Lizzie stood up, flustered. "Sister, I'm sorry, I am." She picked up the book and replaced it on the table, then put her hand on the nun's narrow shoulder. "I'll bring you a lovely slice of bread this afternoon. With plenty of butter. And I'll put jam on it too, if you like, or marmalade. Whatever you'd like."

Sister Antonetta shrugged her off. "I need it now, don't you know!" Her voice was a wail.

"Perhaps we can ask Sister Clementia to fetch you some…"

The nun took a step back. "Sister Clementia?" She squared her shoulders and folded her hands. "You think I'm going to ask one of the lay sisters who isn't even the cook, for a piece of bread? For one thing, I have no permission to speak to her, and she'd have no permission to fetch me anything. For another…." She lowered her voice and looked to the door. "I wouldn't stoop to their level."

Lizzie frowned. "And aren't you all nuns, Sister? Aren't all of you as good as the other?"

The nun stood like a statue, her face stern. "Some of us are more educated and more disciplined than others." She lifted her head and sniffed. "You've been smoking in here, Lizzie."

"Sister, it was just a short break, to give me back and legs a rest. I know I should have gone downstairs for me fag, but…"

"Lizzie." Sister Antonetta looked again to the door. "Do you suppose I might try one?"

It was a moment before Lizzie replied. "D'you mean … a fag?"

Sister Antonetta nodded. Her face brightened. "Just to try it. I've often wondered what it's like to smoke a cigarette."

Lizzie sat down at the table. "Only if you think it's allowed, Sister."

"*Allowed*? And is it up to *you* to question *me* about what's allowed?" Sister Antonetta's face began to gain colour. She stood straight, her face serene. "I'm simply asking you for a favour."

Lizzie drew from her pocket a brown pouch, opened it, and pulled out a thin piece of cigarette paper. She reached into the pouch again, and looking up at the nun, said, "I rolls me own, d'you know that, Sister?"

The nun pursed her lips.

"I mean, I'll have to roll you one too. This isn't a bother to you, Sister? Me licking the paper?"

A muscle flinched on Sister Antonetta's face. "Do what you have to do. I know nothing of these things."

Lizzie plucked some stringy tobacco from the pouch and arranged it on the paper, rolled the paper up, and licked the edge. She tapped it on the table, poked in a stray string of tobacco, and handed it to Sister Antonetta, who sat down at the table across from her. The nun put the cigarette into her mouth. It dangled in front of her chin.

Lizzie rolled one for herself and brought out a box of matches from her pocket. Sister Antonetta thrust her head forward and raised the cigarette.

"You suck in on it, Sister." Lizzie struck a match and held it out to the nun. A flame shot up from the end of the cigarette. She then lit her own. "Suck in, Sister!" she said, waving away the smoke that had risen between them.

Sister Antonetta drew in, and immediately, the cigarette flew out of her mouth onto the table. She doubled over, her body wracked with coughing. A smell of scorched cloth rose from the table.

"Oh, Sister!" Lizzie grabbed hold of a handful of Boston fern, tore it off, picked up the cigarette, and pressed the feathery leaves down on the cloth. "The lovely cloth, look what's happened to it!" She threw the leaves and cigarette, along with her own, onto the dirt of the plant.

Sister Antonetta sat up, her face mottled, and her eyes watering and red-rimmed.

"It's the needlework edging that's got scorched, Sister. Thank God, it's just ash on the table itself." Lizzie rubbed at the table underneath the runner. A light grey smear emerged, dulling the polish. "What are we going to do?"

The nun closed her eyes and heaved a sigh. She looked blankly at the cloth and then up at Lizzie.

The library door opened, and the two looked up to see Reverend Mother standing there, a large, big-boned woman. She carried a folded newspaper. Her face, framed into a large oval by her white linen wimple, appeared weather-beaten, the wrinkles having settled into deep furrows. The two sprang to their feet, and as she did so, Lizzie smoothed the runner over the table's grey patch. Her wiry body was alive and taut.

Sister Antonetta bowed her head and looked at the floor. "Good morning, Mother, good morning."

Reverend Mother let go of the doorknob and came forward. Her walk was slow, but she stood erect, her shoulders stooped only slightly, and she expressed no surprise at the sight of Lizzie and Sister Antonetta. She held out the newspaper and unfolded it. It bore the date, "October 6, 1958."

"Here he is, looking as healthy as can be." Her voice was low in timbre, like a man's. "And now they say he has had a stroke, and...." She looked down at the paper and read: "'... and his condition is grave.'"

Lizzie looked at Sister Antonetta, and when the nun didn't raise her head, she took a halting step forward. "I'm sorry, to be sure, Reverend Mother. Who is this gentleman?"

Reverend Mother continued holding the paper in front of her but made no further move to show it to the other two. Lizzie craned her neck to look at the page.

A photograph in the corner of the page showed Pope Pius XII, his prominent nose in profile, his forehead high beneath a white zucchetto. His right arm was raised in blessing. The headline read, "Pope Seriously Ill."

Lizzie looked up at Reverend Mother, her eyes wide. "Not our Holy Father!"

"After all he's led us through. The voice of God on earth. In grave condition, they say." Reverend Mother stood still, with no expression in her voice.

Sister Antonetta raised her eyes to the newspaper but did not move.

Reverend Mother stepped up to the table, frowned, and tucked the newspaper under her arm. "Who left this book here?" she said, picking up *The Interior Castle*.

"I..." Lizzie began, but Reverend Mother interrupted her.

"Ah yes, Saint Teresa of Avila. Saint Teresa was a mystic and she also had a sense of humour. She was riding her horse one day and fell off, and she looked up to heaven and said, 'Lord, if this is how you treat your friends, no wonder you have so few.'" She looked back and forth between Lizzie and Sister Antonetta. "Saint Teresa wrote this book under obedience. She knew, as we all do, that we must obey our religious superiors in even the smallest thing." She fixed her eyes on the other nun. "To see our superior as the mouthpiece of God, so that nothing is done without the superior's permission. This is what makes saints of us."

"And she had headaches, Mother," Lizzie said. "So it says in the book: 'Weakness in the head.'"

"Yes, I believe she did. Saint Teresa is my patron, and her feast day is coming up next week. Of course, Lizzie, you didn't know me in the days when I was simply Sister Teresa." Reverend Mother returned the book to the table, and as she did so, she noticed the piece of bread lying face-down on the floor and the three scattered pieces of the plate. "What's this?" She stooped to pick up the broken crockery.

Lizzie bent down to the floor. "Please let me, Mother," she said. The nun straightened as Lizzie gathered the pieces and scooped them into her apron. She let out an involuntary groan as she raised herself to her feet. "Reverend Mother, I'm very sorry..." she began.

"What's this bread doing in the library? It has no business being here."

Sister Antonetta stared downward. Lizzie glanced at her and then continued: "Mother, I won't do it again, that is to say, it won't happen again, the bread..."

Reverend Mother was sniffing the air. "You've had your morning break and smoked your cigarette, Lizzie. Good for you. A break is good for us all. Did they make you some tea in the kitchen? Of course, *we* don't eat or drink between meals, but *you* generally have tea in mid-morning, don't you?"

Lizzie said nothing as she placed the bread and the broken pieces of crockery on the scorched edge of the runner.

"Take care you don't spoil my good runner," Reverend Mother said. "I shouldn't take pride in it, for all our things belong to the whole community. This is what our vow of poverty means. Still, that runner was my first piece of cutwork, and it reminds me of my early days."

Lizzie slid along the edge of the table, blocking the nun's view of the runner. "Yes, Mother, I'm sure it's a lovely reminder."

Reverend Mother turned to Sister Antonetta, who lifted the rosary from her side and held on to the crucifix like a prisoner before the scaffold, her eyes downcast. "Why are you in here, Sister?" Reverend Mother narrowed her eyes. Why aren't you at the portress's desk?"

Sister Antonetta's chest moved up and down as she fingered the crucifix. She didn't reply.

"Holy obedience, Sister. This is the bulwark of our life. Obedience separates the wheat from the chaff. You shouldn't have to be reminded."

"Yes, Mother," Sister Antonetta said in a squeak.

Reverend Mother pointed to the bread and crockery pieces. "I'll take those, Lizzie."

"Oh, no, please, Mother. I'll look after..."

"Give them to me, please."

Fumbling, Lizzie picked them up, leaving the edge of the runner exposed, its delicate white stitching now blotted with brown stains. She leaned over the table, as if to cover the spot with her elbow.

"What's this?" Reverend Mother moved along the edge of the table. Lizzie squeezed out of her way. The superior fingered the ruined edge of the runner with her large hand. "Did you do this, Lizzie, with your cigarette?"

"Oh no, I didn't, Mother, that is, it was a mistake, Mother." Lizzie looked over at Sister Antonetta, who had moved to the door, her hand already turning the knob. In an instant, the nun slipped out, as silent as a cat.

Lizzie took a step toward Reverend Mother. "Mother, Sister Antonetta asked me for a fag. She meant no harm. You know how she is, she's just a lovely old soul."

Reverend Mother slid her fingers over the brown edging of the runner.

"She couldn't smoke it, Mother. She coughed it up and it flew over here, and I grabbed it as fast as I could. I'm truly sorry, Mother. I'll mend the runner. I'll get the exact thread and fix it like new."

"Sister Antonetta doesn't have permission to speak to you. Only Sister Clementia has permission to speak to you and only when necessary. Our rule of silence is golden. And you are not to give her anything, Lizzie. Nothing."

"Oh yes, certainly, Mother."

Reverend Mother slipped the newspaper from under her arm and looked down at the pope's picture. "And bring me news of the Holy Father's condition tomorrow, please, Lizzie. A stroke is very serious."

"Yes, Mother, and I'll mend your runner good as new." Holding her apron with its cargo in one hand, Lizzie folded the runner and scooped it up with the other.

"It isn't *my* runner, Lizzie. Haven't I told you that? In religious life, we hold all things in common." She turned to the door.

Lizzie, her hands full, watched her leave.

"Sister, this morning in the library, I saw a book that I thought was about the Sleeping Beauty—you know, that nice story about the princess that gets wakened by the prince when he kisses her? The cover had a picture of a castle, like one of those fairy tales." Lizzie spoke loudly against the furious churning of the laundry's washing machine.

Sister Clementia stood guiding a sheet into the gigantic ironing press, the sleeves of her white work habit rolled to her elbows and her veil tied back between her shoulders. "Did you, Lizzie," she called back.

Lizzie picked up a towel from a mound in the laundry basket and folded it. "I've always loved them stories about princesses. But d'you know what it says on the first page, it says, 'I'm that much beset with headaches that I can't do much of anything else.'"

Sister Clementia blinked through thick spectacles. "Is that so, Lizzie."

"The book was written by Saint Teresa. Did you know, Sister, that Saint Teresa didn't want to write the book because of her headaches, but she did anyway?"

"No, I didn't know that at all."

"Was she a saint because she had headaches and did her work anyway? Then why aren't I a saint?" Lizzie turned to the nun and grinned.

Sister Clementia laughed. "Maybe you are, Lizzie. But isn't God the one that decides?"

"Do you think Reverend Mother is a saint?"

Sister Clementia hesitated. "You have to be dead to be made a saint."

"The Holy Father may soon be a saint, then. Oh, don't get me wrong, Sister. I don't wish him dead." Lizzie made a hasty sign of the cross.

"I'm sure he will be, Lizzie. God help him, that holy man."

"And what about Sister Antonetta?"

Sister Clementia held the corners of a pressed sheet to Lizzie. "What about her?"

The two began to fold the sheet. "Is she saintly? I suppose a nun has to follow the vows. To do everything Reverend Mother says. Is that right, Sister? And if you don't do that, you're not going to be a saint?"

"I suppose so, Lizzie. It's not much of a bother to me."

"Anyway, I'm not soon to be a saint. This morning, I had a fag in the library instead of downstairs. That lovely runner on the table in the library got smudged or something and needs mending. Reverend Mother came in and saw the way it was. I told her I'd fix it, but that was a lie. It's all I can do to darn Frank's socks. The embroidery on that runner is too delicate for me poor fingers. D'you think you or one of the other nuns...?"

"Surely, Lizzie, let me take a look."

Lizzie went to the wall hook where her coat was hanging and took the folded runner from the pocket. The nun ran a reddened, arthritic finger over the edging. "It looks like it may be scorched."

Lizzie turned away. "D'you think so, Sister?"

The nun smiled. "I'll see to it, Lizzie. It will look good as new."

"Oh, and Sister, Reverend Mother said for me to give her news about the Holy Father. But we don't get the newspaper or listen to the radio much, Frank and me. So I don't know how the Holy Father is at all. What shall I tell Reverend Mother about him?"

"Reverend Mother gets the newspaper every day. She told us after breakfast that his condition is very grave. Just say his condition is still grave, the poor man. Coming from yourself, a person who lives in the world outside, she'll think she has the most recent news."

"I seem to be doing things bad, Sister. Fooling Reverend Mother like that, the dear lady. Telling her about Sister Antonetta smoking..." She clapped her hand over her mouth. "I'm not like Saint Teresa at all, except for the headaches."

Through the laundry window, Lizzie saw the short figure of Sister Antonetta picking her way along the gravel drive to the back door of the convent. Looking over at Sister Clementia, who was once again guiding the sheets through the press, she pulled her coat off the wall hook. From the table near the door, she picked up a brown bag and uncurled the top. A sandwich sat inside, freshly wrapped in waxed paper. The thick layer of butter and jam hadn't seeped through. She curled up the bag again. Opening the laundry door, she said, "I'm just off for me afternoon fag, Sister. And when I see Reverend Mother, I'll tell her that the Holy Father is—how is it again?"

"His condition is still grave."

"Right. Still grave."

2. Road to Perfection

THE PAIN GATHERED STRENGTH as Sister Zélie stood waiting before the door. When the bell rang at five minutes to seven, she barely managed to answer it.

"Looks like fine weather again this morning," Father Climacus said, stepping inside. "Another story in Rome, though." He held out a folded newspaper. "They say he's close to death."

He stood waiting for Sister Zélie to lead the way down the corridor to the sacristy beside the chapel, but the wave of pain came again, this time accompanied by another discharge of blood that trickled, warm and sticky, down between her legs. She staggered over to the parlour, grasped the door jamb, and sank onto the nearest chair inside.

"He's in his eighties, so it's to be expected sooner rather than later," the priest continued. When she didn't respond, he looked at her with a slightly puzzled expression through round spectacles. He then turned away, his bald head white and shiny in the subdued light, and disappeared down the corridor to the chapel.

Perspiration gathered on her face, and she ran her finger along the place where the white linen wimple fit against her cheek and underneath the bandeau on her forehead. The sanitary pad was a sodden weight underneath her, but the pain was subsiding somewhat. She eased herself up and took halting steps down the corridor.

The chapel was now fully lit, following the hour-long morning meditation, when only the back light had glowed. A white-veiled novice was lighting the altar candles for Mass. Sister Zélie stood at the chapel entrance for a moment, then turned to the back staircase, stepping down with care. She tightened her buttocks and thighs, as if the soggy mass between her legs might fall away. At the bottom of the staircase, she picked her way through the dim light, holding onto the wall.

In the nuns' washroom, she fumbled for the light switch and stumbled to one of the toilet cubicles. Inside, she pulled up the bulk of her habit skirt and the black-and-white checkered petticoat beneath it, and pulled down her thick knickers. They were already wet and stained with blood. She pulled off the soggy pad, wrapped it in one of the papers in the container attached to the cubicle wall, and dropped it into the waste pail. She grappled through the folds of her habit to her pocket, took out her handkerchief, and wiped her face. The cramps started again, and she leaned forward, pulled her skirt up to her waist, and gazed at the patterns on the linoleum floor. The green-and-brown lines wound in and out and around each other, like the exotic pattern on a Turkish rug. She sat back against the toilet tank and looked at the ceiling, where a faint brown water stain ran in a fluid line from the wall to a point outside her vision. Eventually, the pain began to subside and she took a fresh pad from the container, and then a second one, and adjusted them onto her sanitary belt. She pulled up her knickers, dropped her skirt, then stood upright and squared her shoulders.

Upstairs, standing outside the chapel door, she watched the last of the nuns returning from the communion rail. Father Climacus had turned back up the steps to the altar, his stiff white vestment like a wall facing the rows of nuns. The Mass was nearly over. Sister Zélie hesitated at the door. In the front rows knelt the novices, their white veils falling like curtains, and behind them, the lay sisters. And then, in order of their age in religious life, the rest of the professed nuns. Her own space stood vacant, a rupture in the ordered structure. And in the last row, Reverend Mother knelt alone, her head slightly bowed. Her elbows, uncharacteristically, leaned against the pew in front of her. Sister Zélie moved carefully up the side aisle and knelt at her own place. The heavy bleeding had not started up again.

As soon as the priest began the Last Gospel, the two kitchen sisters got up from their places, genuflected, and left. Sister Zélie followed, as she always did, to prepare the priest's breakfast tray. She had been in chapel less than three minutes. As she passed Reverend Mother, she bowed in the usual manner. The superior regarded her with an impassive expression. Sister Zélie took a quick intake of breath.

At the back staircase, she grabbed hold of the rail to keep herself steady. Downstairs in the kitchen, the two cooks were fastening white aprons over their habits and tying their veils behind their shoulders as they bustled around the stove. Sister Zélie surveyed the contents of the priest's tray on the sideboard: the silver cutlery, the china cup and saucer, the crystal marmalade dish. The bread was already toasting.

She leaned heavily against the sideboard as pain crashed through her. One of the cooks, whose name was Sister Kate, whispered in a hurried voice, "Toast, egg and bacon, marmalade, coffee, cream. There you go now, Zelly."

Sister Zélie picked up the tray and staggered, tipping it to one side. The cook steadied it with her hand. "Are you all right, Sister?"

She nodded, and with concentrated effort, held the tray steady and left the kitchen. A wave of nausea engulfed her as she climbed the back staircase, balancing the tray in one hand while clutching the rail. The dishes slipped to one side, coffee spilling from the small pot onto the cloth underneath.

Upstairs, she knocked on the door of the parlour and softly opened it. The priest was sitting at the table in a leather chair, reading the newspaper. He held the paper to one side and said nothing as she placed the tray in front of him. "I'm sorry, Father," she began. The nausea rose once again, and she gasped in a whisper, "I spilled the coffee."

"Already they're talking about the next pope," the priest said, folding back the newspaper and regarding the breakfast tray. "Poor man's not even dead yet."

Sister Zélie backed away and held onto a chair near the parlour door.

The priest took a bite of toast and spoke into the newspaper. "He might have a sickbed consistory, make more cardinals. Unlikely, though. Everything's failing. Brain hemorrhage, lungs, heart—everything's running down fast." He put the paper down and picked up his knife and fork.

The room was silent except for the sound of cutlery against the priest's breakfast plate. Sister Zélie bowed and left the parlour.

When she reached the nuns' refectory, the others were already seated in silence, the only sound that of spoons against egg cups. Plates of bread were passed down each side of the horseshoe-shaped table. Reverend Mother sat at the head, where the silverware and china dishes were similar to those on the priest's tray, as was the crystal marmalade dish and the toast plate.

Sister Zélie looked down at her egg and another wave of nausea overcame her. A plate of bread was passed to her. She scanned the plate and pulled out a thin slice that she broke into two pieces. From one piece, she broke off part of the crust and took a small bite, chewing slowly as she looked again at the egg. She took up the spoon to crack it, then put it down again.

Reverend Mother laid her napkin on the table, and the nun sitting on her left rolled it up and fastened a silver napkin ring around it. The superior spoke into the silence. "Our Holy Father is now paralyzed and is in a coma. It appears he's dying. We must intensify our prayers." She stood up, and as she did so, the rest of the nuns rose, their chairs scraping against the floor. Passing Sister Zélie, she looked at the nun's napkin, still pinned to the top part of her habit, and then at the unbroken egg. "You've eaten nothing, Sister," she said.

Sister Zélie swallowed the bread. "No, Mother," she whispered.

"Sit down, and eat your egg." Reverend Mother's face, weather-worn and the colour of a cardboard box, remained expressionless.

Sister Zélie sat and cracked open her egg. The top fell onto the plate, white and gelatinous, as nausea rose again. There was silence as the nuns remained standing at their places, their eyes lowered. One of them furtively pushed her napkin into its holder.

"Pass her the bread," the superior continued. "Take another slice. We must have strong and healthy nuns. This is a matter of obedience."

The nun beside her made a space beside Sister Zélie's place and set down the bread plate. Sister Zélie reached for another slice.

Reverend Mother turned and left the room, and the other nuns dispersed in silence. When all were turned to the door, their backs to Sister Zélie, she put the slice back onto the bread plate. A minute later, the refectory was empty except for Sister Zélie and Sister Kate, who had stayed on to clear the tables. Tying her blue apron around her waist, she approached Sister Zélie. "You're pale, Zelly. Tell Reverend Mother you're sick. Go on now." She looked to the door. "I'll take care of this." She whisked Sister Zélie's dishes over to the refectory sideboard.

Outside the refectory, Sister Zélie saw Reverend Mother standing in the alcove where the statue of St. Anne with the young Mary stood. As she bowed to the superior, Reverend Mother beckoned to her. "An obedient nun doesn't need to be told to eat," she said.

Sister Zélie's eyes became unfocused. She reached for the wall for support.

"Where were you during Mass? You didn't even receive Communion."

"Mother, I was feeling sick. I'm sorry. After I let the priest in, I had to go to the bathroom. I didn't realize how long I was in there."

Reverend Mother's face didn't change nor did she speak.

Sister Zélie continued in a low voice: "It's my monthly period. It's been getting worse."

"What kind of nonsense is that? Every woman has monthly episodes, and everyone learns to offer them up as a sacrifice. To miss Holy Mass without permission is unthinkable. You may kneel before the community at supper."

"Mother, it's just that I wondered if it may be abnormal..."

"Think of someone else for once. Think of our Holy Father. He's suffering for the whole Church. You should be praying for him instead of feeling sorry for yourself."

Reverend Mother turned away and walked down the corridor to the staircase, her shoulders stooped somewhat, a recent departure from the erect posture that had always been her hallmark.

The blood hadn't come with the same savage pain and discharge that she had felt earlier in the morning, but when she checked it in the bathroom, she saw that it had seeped all the way through the first pad and had begun to dot the second. She sat back, a feeling of physical weakness overtaking her, and doubled over again as the sharpness of the pain returned. On the patterned linoleum beneath her, the green-and-brown lines slithered like snakes around each other. When the pain subsided again, she looked at her pocket watch. The time was nudging toward eight thirty. She sat up and with shaking hands affixed new pads to the sanitary belt and left the bathroom.

Outside in the corridor, she heard behind her a whisper: "Zélie!" Sister Clementia stood against the wall, looking up and down the corridor through thick spectacles. Sister Zélie put her finger to her lips. The other nun beckoned her over to the broom closet near the bathroom. "Just for a minute, Sister," she whispered as she opened the door and they both crowded inside. Sister Clementia pulled the door until only a thin shaft of light sliced into the small space. She took from her pocket a wrinkled cloth that had been neatly folded. "Can you do something with this?" she whispered.

"What do you mean?" Sister Zélie whispered back. The close smell of dust from the mops and brooms caught in her nostrils, and she put her hand up to her nose.

The other nun spoke in anxious gasps. "It's Reverend Mother's runner from the library table. The edging got burnt. I can't mend it, not with my hands. Please, Zelly, will you fix it?"

Sister Zélie took the cloth from the other nun's shaking hand. It swam in front of her as nausea rose in waves. She pushed open the broom closet door. "Sorry, Clemmie. I just have to get out of here."

Still inside the closet, Sister Clementia whispered loudly, "Zelly, are you feeling sick?"

Sister Zélie put her finger to her lips, turned back, and stood in the doorway facing the other nun. "Clemmie, how can I get through the day? Eight French classes. I just don't know."

The other nun blinked through her thick spectacles and said nothing.

In the nuns' common room, Sister Zélie placed the runner on her desk and picked up her battered briefcase from the chair.

In her office, Reverend Mother stood before her wooden desk. On the desk was a green ink blotter and a black stand-up crucifix with a sagging, flesh-coloured corpus and drops of red paint about the hands and feet. Facing her across the desk stood Sister Antonetta, whose short stature was emphasized by the superior's height. She stood motionless, except for the occasional twitch of a finger, her hands folded at her waist.

"There's a softening of the spirit in this community," Reverend Mother said. "Among the younger nuns. No understanding of penance and mortification. Wanting sympathy when they should be sacrificing themselves."

Sister Antonetta shook her head and clucked her tongue.

Reverend Mother swept her hand across the newspaper that lay on the desk. "All this, while our Holy Father is hovering between life and death," she continued. "She whimpers and says she's in pain. What does she want? An easy life?"

"Awful, Mother," Sister Antonetta murmured.

"Doesn't she know after all this time that an easy life is the last thing you'll find here? We're seeking perfection. And the road to perfection is a road of suffering. That's what *The Imitation of Christ* says, and there is no saint who would tell you otherwise. We carry our suffering with patience and forbearance."

She picked up the crucifix from the desk and rubbed her thumb along the feet of the corpus. "We suffer with Him to the death. And she whines because of a bit of pain."

Sister Antonetta shook her head with more vigour and frowned. "Oh, Mother."

"You must tell me if you see that she's doing anything against our Holy Rule. For you, of course, that would be an act of charity. It would be a help to her, to have it pointed out."

"Yes, Mother." The nun's face brightened. "Those kitchen goings-on are a disgrace…"

"Not the kitchen nuns. The other ones. At St. Monica's. That one in particular." Reverend Mother gestured to the window.

Sister Antonetta's smile turned into a puzzled frown. "The school, Mother?"

"Yes, the school."

"But, Mother, I have no reason to go to St. Monica's."

"We'll find a way for you to go there in obedience."

The nun smiled again. "Oh yes, Mother."

Reverend Mother walked over to a bookcase behind Sister Antonetta and pulled down a large volume. "This is so heavy, I have to carry it in both hands."

"It looks like a beautiful book, Mother."

"It's all about our Holy Father." She turned the book so that the front was facing Sister Antonetta. The cover photograph showed Pope Pius XII wearing a white cape against a rich red brocade background, his right hand raised in blessing, an ornate ring on his third finger. "There are some books that are too precious to be placed in the library. This is one of them." She put the book on the desk and turned some of the pages. "Here he is as a young priest. Look at his delicate face. That noble nose. Look at those slender hands. So sensitive. Already a holy man."

Sister Antonetta leaned across the desk and peered at the photograph. Reverend Mother turned to her. "Have you no work to do? Go away with you now."

Sister Zélie sat at the teacher's desk, staring blankly into space as the girls spilled through the door. The usual buzz filled the room, some of the students chatting to one another across rows. Sally Sullivan opened her notebook to a clean page.

"What's the date?" she asked no one in particular.

"The seventh," someone called back.

She flipped back a few pages and wrote: "7 *octobre* 1958." She sat back, absently twirling a lock of hair.

Behind her, Gwen was reading aloud: "'Ah, oh, uh. Ah, oh, uh.' Okay, it says, 'the lips progressively protrude. The jaw narrows and the tongue rises.' Uh, is this a French *textbook* or is it about French something else?" An embarrassed giggle sounded around her. She went on: "I mean, not about the French *language*."

A whisper came from the next row: "Ha ha. We get it, Gwen. Just shut up."

Sally turned around furtively. "Shush, she'll *hear* you."

Gwen called out: "Hey, Sister, how come you're not writing the quiz on the blackboard? And I studied last night too!"

Sister Zélie didn't reply.

"She looks pale," Sally whispered.

"She's always pale," Gwen whispered back. "Maybe it's because her eyebrows are so thick and black."

The chatter around the room subsided as the girls looked to Sister Zélie. "*Cinquième leçon*," she said finally, without enthusiasm.

"Aren't we going to pray first, Sister?" a girl in the front row asked. "We always pray first."

"Yes, all right," Sister Zélie said. The girls stared at her as she leaned her hands on the desk and stood up like an old woman and began the prayer: "*Au nom du Père et du Fils et du Saint-Esprit....*"

She seated herself at the desk after the prayer had ended instead of remaining on her feet as she usually did. There was a quiet murmur in the classroom as the girls looked around at each other.

Gwen whispered to Sally's back: "How come she's not walking around up there like she always does?"

"Maybe she's not feeling well," Sally said over her shoulder.

"Maybe it's her..." Gwen giggled. "Do nuns have periods?"

Sally turned halfway around. "Stop it! Just shush!"

The nun said in a dull voice, "*Cinquième leçon*, please. Page eighteen."

Gwen flipped through the pages. "You mean, *page dix-huit*, Sister. We speak French in this class, *n'est-ce pas?*"

Sister Zélie passed her hand over her face. "All right, just say it after me. *Je regarde la photographie de la tour Eiffel.*"

Around the room, the girls opened their textbooks to a photograph of the soaring grey tower. Sally smoothed out the page, then turned to the front cover of the book. There, a similar photograph showed the Eiffel Tower rising into the clouds, with the blue sky stretching into the distance. She held up the book, pointing to a monument in front of the tower, and turned back to Gwen. "What's this?"

"Looks like a bunch of people in a jumble," Gwen whispered.

"A jumble of people made of stone." Sally turned back to the other page.

At the head of the room, Sister Zélie looked into space as some of the girls at the front continued reading aloud: *"Je montre les photographies à Jean. J'étudie la leçon..."*

Gwen poked Sally in the back. "What're you doing this weekend?"

Sally looked up at Sister Zélie. The nun's head was drooping. She turned to Gwen. "I think something's wrong with her."

Just then, there was a loud cry at the front of the room: "Sister!"

The girls jumped to their feet and strained forward. Sister Zélie was slumped over the teacher's desk, her wimple and veil hiding her face completely, the pages of the open textbook crushed under her chest.

"I'm getting Sister Martha!" Sally called as she sprinted out the door, her brown ponytail flying behind her, the skirt of her maroon uniform flapping against the door frame. When she returned a moment later, a circle of girls was pressed in around Sister Zélie. Sister Martha rushed in behind, her face flushed and her double chin quivering. She pushed the students aside. "Let me through!" she said.

Sally stood behind Sister Zélie and took hold of her shoulders from behind. "Sister, can you lift yourself up?"

"Don't touch her!" Sister Martha bellowed.

"I'm just trying to..." Sally protested.

"I said, don't touch her!" Sister Martha elbowed Sally out of the way and stopped at the sight of the nun collapsed in front of her. She looked around, as if not sure of what to do. "Just leave her. I'm getting Sister Beatrice." Her bulky figure disappeared out the door.

Gwen pushed through the crowd and stood beside the nun. "We should find out if she's alive or dead," she said.

"Don't *say* such a thing!" Sally placed a tentative finger on one of Sister Zélie's hands. The hand slid along the surface of the desk, and Sister Zélie lifted her head, her eyes fluttering. The girls leaned forward in hushed silence.

When Sister Beatrice, the principal, appeared, straight-backed and calmly authoritative, the girls shrank away, making a pathway for her. She bent over the stricken nun.

"What happened?" Sister Zélie croaked. "The pain...."

Sister Beatrice looked around at the girls. "Class dismissed now," she said in a low, stern voice. "Gather up your books, go to the auditorium, and wait for the bell for the next class."

As the other girls emptied out of the room, Gwen took her time gathering her books together. Sally stood in the doorway, her eyes on Sister Zélie. She shifted her books from one arm to the other. Gwen joined her, and as they passed through the cloakroom, Gwen said, "I hope she'll be all right. Let's see what they're going to do." She pointed to the cloakroom's far corner.

Sally held back and tugged on her ponytail.

Gwen slipped to the corner. "C'mon."

Sally looked at the door, hesitant, then followed.

At the classroom doorway, Sister Beatrice was saying to Sister Martha, "Tell Reverend Mother that Zélie needs an ambulance!"

"You know what she'll say to me. She'll say, 'Give her a tonic.' You're best to go yourself."

"All right, I'll presume permission. I'll call an ambulance myself."

Sister Beatrice ran from the room, her footsteps echoing down the hall. When she returned, the two girls shrank against the corner of the cloakroom.

Sister Beatrice said, passing into the classroom, "They'll be here in five minutes." She stopped to catch her breath. "We have to give her space to breathe. Make her more comfortable."

Gwen tiptoed to the doorway and beckoned to Sally. The two girls watched as the principal reached for Sister Zélie's veil and removed the black-headed pin that held it in place. The veil fell away, revealing a white undercap and cloth strip holding the white forehead bandeau tight around the head. Sister Martha lifted the bandeau, untied the wimple, and loosened the ties of the close-fitting undercap.

A siren sounded in the distance and gradually came closer until its shrillness reverberated through the silent school and came to a whirring stop. Sister Beatrice shot out of the room, her black habit skirt whipping behind her. She returned, followed by two ambulance men in blue uniforms who marched into the room bearing a stretcher, which they set on the floor. There were whispers and murmurings between the men. Then, getting on each side of Sister Zélie, they lifted her from the chair. She groaned, and her eyelids fluttered. As they set her down on the stretcher, her undercap drooped open. It then fell off, revealing a shaved head. Sister Martha moved to place it back on the nun's head, but one of the men brushed her aside. The two worked quickly, without speaking or looking at the nuns. One of them pulled a blanket over Sister Zélie and tucked it around her neck. Only her shorn head could be seen. Together, they lifted the stretcher and carried it through the door. As they passed through the cloakroom, one of them said, "Which hospital are we taking him to?"

The two girls, still huddled in the corner, stared at the parting stretcher and Sister Zélie's exposed, shaved head. Gwen put her hand to her mouth and gasped. "They think she's a man!" she whispered.

Lizzie hesitated before the closed door of Reverend Mother's office. She moved her lips with concentration and ran her fingers over her hair, then leaned her mop against the wall and knocked on the door.

"Come in," a deep voice said.

Inside, Reverend Mother sat at her desk. Before her, the large book with pictures of the pope was propped open. Lizzie stood in the doorway and bowed.

"Yes, Lizzie, what is it?"

"Reverend Mother, you wanted to know how the Holy Father is. His condition is grave, Reverend Mother."

"Yes, I know that. I've been reading a book about him. He was a diplomat, you know. He was very much against the Communists. *Is*, I mean. He may rally yet. We must pray for him." Her facial features softened as she spoke.

"Oh, yes, Mother." Lizzie bobbed her head. "Me and Sister Clementia, we've been saying the rosary in the laundry for him. And..."

Reverend Mother was looking beyond her, to where Sister Beatrice had appeared in the corridor outside. Her face changed expression. "Thank you, Lizzie. That will be all."

Lizzie bowed and left as Sister Beatrice entered the office and bowed.

"Yes, Sister, what is it?"

"Mother, it's Sister Zélie. She's been taken to the hospital. She collapsed in the classroom."

"The hospital? How did she get to the hospital?"

"I was afraid for her life, and I decided there was no time to come over here and ask for your permission to call an ambulance." Sister Beatrice's face was flushed.

"You called an ambulance? Without permission?"

"I presumed permission. Mother, it was serious..."

"Yes, I know it was serious. It was a serious matter that you should take such decisions into your own hands. You are the principal of St. Monica's only because of holy obedience, do you not remember that? There's a low element entering this community. A spirit of defiance. We must renew our submission to the superior of the community as the voice of God's will. You will kneel and ask forgiveness now and will do so again before supper in front of the community."

"Yes Mother." Sister Beatrice knelt and made the sign of the cross. "Reverend Mother," she began. "I accuse myself of acting against the Holy Rule by calling an ambulance for Sister Zélie without permission. By doing this, I failed against holy obedience. I beg your forgiveness, and I ask that, in your charity, you pray for me so that I may become more obedient and better observe the Holy Rule."

Sister Martha stood at the door of the school facing the convent. Opening it, she saw Gwen and Sally sitting on the steps.

Sally looked up. "Sister, will she be all right? I mean, Sister Zélie?"

"She's in God's hands, and so are we all. That's all I know. Pray for her."

"Good thing the ambulance got here. Do you think she would have died if it hadn't got here in time?"

"That's hard to say. Thank God Sister Beatrice acted quickly." She turned to them. "How do you know about the ambulance?"

Gwen stood up. "Sister, don't nuns have hair?" Sally poked her, and Gwen winced. "I mean, do you, do they shave their heads?"

"That is none of your business." Sister Martha's tone was sharp. She was already at the gate leading to the convent.

"Sister, shaved heads are supposed to be a sign of shame, aren't they? What do nuns have to be ashamed about?"

The nun disappeared behind the hedge.

3. Vocation

THE CONVERTIBLE J.J. DROVE WAS PARKED exactly where she'd said it would be, along the curb outside the dentist's office. Except that now, the top was down and that little madam, Gwen, had joined J.J. in the front seat, the two girls displayed for all the world to see. No mistaking the maroon uniforms and cream cardigans of St. Monica's. And there, leaning against the car with their hands in their pockets, acting as if they belonged, stood three St. Paul's boys.

Frowning, Sister Martha stepped out from the building's revolving door. She was in no mood for teenage high jinks. When J.J. had dropped her off here, Sister Martha had suggested the girl drive the short distance to the public library and get started on her homework. Then you'd think she'd have waited discreetly inside the car after returning, especially knowing that Sister Martha would emerge from the dentist's office with a swollen cheek and a sore mouth. *That would have been the decent, common-sense thing to do, wouldn't it? But no, not Snow White. Let's pick up Rose Red, let's put the top down on this summery October afternoon and watch the boys collect around. Bees to blossoms.*

The top was back on, though, when she reached the car, and she saw Gwen scramble into the back. The lace of her slip, the top of her stockings, and even a garter, all in full view of the boys. *Wouldn't the sensible thing—not to mention the modest thing—have been to open the door, get out of the car, open the back door, and climb back in? Wouldn't it have been? But for our madam the sensible, or the modest? Hardy har har, as they are all saying these days.*

At least the boys, thanks be to God, had the common decency to melt away as Sister Martha walked to the car. "Hi, Sister," one of them mumbled as he opened the car door for her. There was a young-manliness about him, with his sheepish blush, the school tie loosened at his throat, his long stride, his strong hand on the door handle. It was easy to see why the girls would want to flaunt themselves.

"*Semper ubi sub ubi*, Sister," Gwen said from the back seat. "See, we've been studying our Latin."

Sister Martha frowned, puzzled. "'Always where under where...?'"

"Get it, Sister?" Gwen bobbed her head in-between the front seats. Her hair was dark and short, with a metallic auburn tint. Some girls simply did not know how to leave well enough alone; they insisted on cheapening themselves. "'Always wear underwear.' You never know."

Sister Martha's frozen face prevented her from smiling, as she might have done otherwise, at the girl's breeziness. She often found herself grinning at a racy comment from girls like Gwen when she should have maintained a stern expression.

She stared straight ahead as J.J. started up the car. "How was it, Sister?" J.J. asked.

"It was my penance for the day." She felt embarrassed at having to speak out of one side of her mouth, her cheek bulging against the stiff wimple around her face.

J.J.'s plump little cheeks spread into a slow smile. She really was a sweet thing, with her blonde curly hair and her lightly freckled nose. Not like madam there in the back seat.

"Let's see what you look like." It was the peanut gallery behind her.

Sister Martha turned and came face to face with the girl, whose tinted strands of hair fell across her cheek. Her eyes were so brown you couldn't make out the pupils. She hated to admit how much the dark centres of those eyes unnerved her. She never knew when Gwen was serious. She often wondered if the little live wire was making fun of her. Sister Martha gave her a full-face stare. Let her have some of her own back. "There, madam," she said, staring right into those dark centres. "Are you satisfied?" She felt ridiculous and ashamed at her display of impatience, especially with her face the way it was, like a pig on a platter with an apple in its mouth. The cavity had been deep, and the sound of the drill, blasting inside her mouth, had gone on and on, the pain lashing through her in spite of the anaesthetic. She had tried to say a silent prayer—"For love of Thee," or some such thing—but the words felt limp and empty. She couldn't even pray properly.

"Don't worry Sister," Gwen said. Her head bobbed forward between the two front seats. "It happens to the best of us."

"The best of us?" Saliva sprayed from her distorted mouth. She hoped Gwen would take her outburst as a joke. There was always a teasing rapport between herself and certain girls. The feisty ones. In fact, of all the girls that passed through her hands year by year, these were the ones she liked best. The girls with daring and spunk, and yes, it was true—her favourites were those with a hint of irreverence about them, who chewed gum during Mass and wrapped it in Kleenex before going to Communion.

"You'll live," Gwen said, settling back. "But Sister, let's say you don't live. I mean, let's say you get taken sick tomorrow. Like Sister Zélie did yesterday. Let's say someone puts poison in your food. Do we get a spare during Latin?"

Sister Martha jabbed the air with her forefinger. "Homework done by tomorrow at eleven-ten! On the dot!"

J.J. drove with ease, smoothly steering the car, an expert driver already. Her father had given her this yellow convertible during the summer, as a present for her sixteenth birthday.

She had received special permission to park it at the school and in exchange had agreed to do errands for the nuns. She now turned onto a tree-lined street. They drove in silence for a few seconds, Gwen settling herself in the back and humming tunelessly.

J.J. reached for the car radio. "Let's have some real music." Sister Martha saw her smile at Gwen in the rear-view mirror. She punched a button, and a wailing woman's voice filled the car. Gwen gave a whoop and joined in off-key: "'*Who's sorry now, whose heart is ach-ing for break-ing each vow....*'"

"You're ruining it!" J.J. switched off the radio.

"I like that song!" Gwen shot forward and switched it back on. The wailing continued: "'*You had your way, now you must pay....*'"

It was at moments like this—sitting in a car, listening to a popular song on the radio, driving down a street where the houses stood side by side, where people sat at kitchen tables and looked out upon back gardens and carried on conversations—that Sister Martha realized she truly lived in a different world. A world where there were no houses, but only a convent with long corridors, where meals took place at a long table and one of the nuns read aloud the life of a saint while the rest ate in silence, looking down at their plates. She dreaded these excursions, these trips to the doctor or dentist. More than anything else, it was dislocating to look at the houses. She could put up with the embarrassment of loosening her wimple at the throat as she sat in the dentist's chair, her thick black shoes sticking up in the air as if she were a corpse in a cartoon. She could put up with the pain and discomfort. But she was unable to pray as well as she should on these occasions, and once back inside the convent, met by the silence and the smell of floor polish and boiled meat, she felt strangely out of place.

"Wow, Sister, can you believe it?" J.J. said. "The pope!"

Sister Martha gave a start; she had been lost in her own

thoughts, oblivious to the droning voice that had followed the song on the radio. J.J. turned up the volume, but the announcer had gone on to other matters.

She switched off the radio. "They said he's dying." Her face was flushed. "What do you think's going to happen now?"

Sister Martha said nothing. This morning, Reverend Mother had told the community after breakfast that the pope was near death. "Satan tries to worm his way into the hearts and souls of those specially chosen by God, and who knows the tremendous struggle that might be going on for possession of this most holy of all souls?" Reverend Mother had gone on like this from the head of the table while the nuns sat in stillness, Sister Martha looking at the apple peels on her plate and planning her first period class.

"It's hard to believe, isn't it?" J.J. kept her eyes straight ahead, her hand on the top of the steering wheel, neither tight nor loose, but almost casual.

"The poor pope," Gwen said in a subdued voice.

Sister Martha sensed that the girls seemed to want her to say something. "Yes, it is hard to believe." She tried summoning up more. Pope Pius XII had led the Church for so long, all through the war, through the struggle against Communism. It seemed as if he should go on forever being the shepherd of souls. "You wonder who can fill his shoes. I know there are many holy men among the cardinals, but..." She could think of nothing else to say. She felt tired and overwhelmed. Her mouth was a swollen mass, and the pain throbbed. She wanted to go to bed, and it crossed her mind now that she might put the case to Reverend Mother. She would wear a pathetic expression and perhaps try to emphasize the swelling by twisting her mouth further to one side. She might slur her words, and perhaps let her head droop. Reverend Mother had a heart of stone, but she just might have pity given the recent unhappy news about the pope.

"Sister, is the pope always for life?" J.J asked.

"Of course. It's the highest vocation in the Church. God doesn't just offer a vocation for a few years. It's forever."

"What if he loses his marbles? Goes senile?" Gwen was once again bobbing up and down.

"Never worry. The pope will always speak the truth on matters of faith and morals. Think of the popes of the Middle Ages. Some of them were reprehensible, but when they spoke in matters of doctrine, they spoke absolute truth."

"What does 'reprehensible' mean?" Trust Gwen to pick up on such a word. Sister Martha regretted mentioning the bad popes, but inevitably, every year in religion class, one of the cleverer girls always brought a question up: "What about those popes who had mistresses?" Or: "Is it true that a pope once made his dog a cardinal?" Hearing such questions, the bored madams like Gwen shot their heads up, wide-eyed.

She turned her head away and looked at the leaves on the sidewalk, most yellow, some already brown. Autumn was her favourite time of the year, the days still sunny. By October, the shock of yet another school year was over, and she had welcomed back the old students and was beginning to know the new girls by name. Some of them were beauties like Gwen; some were pleasant and gentle, like J.J.; others, she was ashamed to admit, were bland and forgettable.

"What part of the city do you live in, J.J.?" She surprised herself at the question. The nuns had been taught from earliest years to show no curiosity in the girls. They were teachers, after all, not friends. There was always the great danger of favourites. And so the girls' families were mysteries. The nuns were encouraged, however, to keep an eye open for promising candidates for the novitiate, and Sister Martha had such an eye on J.J.

"The Belmont district," J.J. said. Sister Martha had no idea what part of the city Belmont was in. She had only ever travelled the route from the train station to the convent and the half-block-long walk from the school to Purification of

Our Lady Church. And, of course, the unusual forays to the doctor and dentist.

She waited for J.J. to say more, but the girl just kept on driving, her left hand on the top of the steering wheel, her right on the side, the cuffs of her cream sweater neatly rolled back. Her hands were healthy and firm, young hands. They remained on the wheel exactly so when she stopped for a red light. Her hair was short and curled around her ears, but did dark roots seem to be showing? Who coloured their hair was a common topic of conversation among the girls. With some, the artificial colour was obvious, but Sister Martha didn't want to believe it of J.J.

She had never met a nicer girl than J.J. A natural upturn at the corners of her mouth gave her face a perpetually smiling look. She seemed to regard everyone equally: Sister Beatrice the principal, Mr. Walenski the janitor, and everyone in-between, even the girls of questionable character. For all, the upturned mouth and a pleasant remark. J.J. would make a splendid nun. She wasn't the brightest spark in Latin class—she didn't know the difference between accusative and dative, and she couldn't translate the simplest of sentences from Julius Caesar's *De Bello Gallico*. But of course, none of this mattered when it came to vocation. God could choose whom He liked. And Sister Martha became convinced that He was calling J.J.

But did J.J. relish the thought of a religious vocation? Sister Martha wasn't sure. She remembered the first day of school last year, when she had read off the list of class names. "Jennifer Jones." A soft titter had run across the room. "Sawng of Bern-a-*dette*," one girl sang out tunelessly.

"Jennifer Jones?" Sister Martha repeated, looking around the class, at first puzzled and then annoyed. She always bristled at any hint that the class might slip out of her control. Her eyes followed the turned heads to the girl with the short blonde hair sitting halfway down the far left row. The girl's face had

turned blotchy red, her look of discomfort so acute that Sister
Martha quickly looked away. She kept reading down the roll,
not wanting to single out the embarrassed girl further.

She needn't have worried. After class, she turned from the
blackboard to see J.J. standing in front of her. The girl was
composed, her face open and confident. "Sister, my name really
is Jennifer, but I'm called J.J."

Sister Martha fumbled with the blackboard brush and put
it back on the ledge and wiped the chalk dust from her hands
with her handkerchief. The girl's composure unnerved her. She
tried to sound brisk. "Fine. Then, that's what I'll call you."

The girl kept on in a friendly voice: "Last year, I had a pyjama
party and we were all in my bedroom, eating potato chips and
horsing around, and we decided to watch the late-night movie
on my TV. It was black and white and *ancient*—made in 1943,
so it said at the end. It was called *The Song of Bernadette*. It
was all about a girl who saw visions of Our Lady on a rock
at Lourdes, and then water gushed up miraculously from the
rock. Do you know about her, Sister?"

Sister Martha smiled at the girl's naiveté, and nodded.

J.J. went on: "Anyway, her name was Bernadette, and she
became a nun. The name of the actress who played her was
Jennifer Jones, and as soon as the others saw her name, they
all began teasing me." She shifted her books, put the palms
of her hands together, and continued in a mock-pious voice:
"'Jennifer Jones! Ho-ly St. Ber-na-dette! A *nun!*' We ended
up having a pillow fight, and I won—well, it was *my* pyjama
party—and I made them promise not to call me 'Jennifer' again.
So, that's why I'm J.J."

Sister Martha was speechless. She tried to visualize the mild
J.J. in a pretty bedroom full of knick-knacks and fluffy things.
A bedroom that contained, of all things, a television. The kind
of bedroom that would test a girl's vocation. It was easier,
perhaps, when you lived in a modest house in the country
and shared a bedroom with two sisters as she herself had.

In fact, *The Song of Bernadette* had been a deciding factor in Sister Martha's own vocation. Could it have been as long as fifteen years ago? She remembered the lovely young actress, dressed to play a sickly peasant girl, but looking lithe and pretty. She recalled the scene where the girl was crossing a stream with the help of a neighbour boy who clearly had his eye on her and no idea what was in store. As a girl, Sister Martha had pictured herself as Bernadette, long-legged, calm, and soft-spoken even when treated harshly in the convent. Then had come the shock of looking in the mirror afterwards at her own round face and pudgy body. Sister Martha brought her thoughts back to the present as J.J.'s voice came from behind the steering wheel. "I know he's an old man, but surely he can't possibly die," she was saying. "We haven't known any other pope."

"He's the most holy of souls," Sister Martha said. She closed her eyes. Her mouth felt like it was packed with cotton, and the throbbing pounded inside her head. She was starting to spout Reverend Mother's gibberish, and so it was time to keep silent. Not that it was gibberish to say that the pope was the most holy of souls, of course, but she felt awkward speaking to the girls like that. She would best keep her dignity by fingering the rosary that hung from her waist. This small action would prevent her from exposing any more of her foolishness. She picked up her rosary and rubbed one bead with her thumb. What would she say to her classes when he died? Please God, he would rally to continue leading the Church. Could popes really go senile? Dear God, it was blasphemous to think of such things.

"Sister?' It was the peanut gallery again, speaking from the back seat.

She turned slightly. "I was praying," she said. "Saying my rosary."

"Do we get extra marks on our next exam for picking you up at the dentist?"

Sister Martha kept her voice clipped. "You come along for the ride, miss, when you should be at home doing your homework, and there you are flirting on the street with the boys. And J.J., what were you thinking, bringing her along?" She heard the edge as she spoke, and it occurred to her that she had been hoping for the opportunity to be alone with J.J., to broach the subject of a religious vocation.

They turned a corner, and the solid red brick of Purification Church came into view. "Pure Vacation," some of the students called the church, especially when classes were cancelled because of a school Mass. Along the street, girls in the familiar maroon uniforms sauntered in twos and threes. Laggards, probably. Late detentions. Some talking to boys. St. Paul's Boys' School was several blocks away, yet the boys always seemed to appear whenever any girls were leaving St. Monica's.

J.J. brought the car to a stop at the convent's back gate and high wall. Sister Martha opened the door and stepped out.

"See you tomorrow Sister," the girls called. She turned to wave and saw Gwen flipping over into the front seat, her legs and slip on full display. Then, the girl waved with a big smile. At least, if nothing else, Gwen didn't seem to carry a grudge. All that was visible of J.J. was her sweatered sleeve and her hand turning the steering wheel as the car moved away from the curb. Sister Martha looked over at the chapel windows. A few were open because of the unusually fine weather. She felt suspended between two worlds.

In a way, she was glad to get back. Much more time spent in the world and you could really slack off, become worldly. She was already inclined in that direction as it was, as Reverend Mother never tired of telling her.

Once inside, she withdrew her watch from a small pocket inside the folds of her habit. Quarter to five. Normally, she would be in school, marking or supervising detentions, but here she was, with time on her hands. Unheard of. She heard sounds from the kitchen, dishes rattling and general busyness, and she stopped in front of the doorway.

Inside, Sister Catherine—or Sister Kate as some of them called her, although never in Reverend Mother's presence—was tasting something from a pot on the stove. She motioned to a white-veiled novice and shook a giant salt shaker at her. "It wants salt, Sister," she whispered. The novice bowed her head and came over to the stove.

Sister Kate looked up and saw Sister Martha standing in the doorway. She gave a sympathetic smile and hurried over. Sister Kate had to walk a fine line in the kitchen, observing the strict rule of silence when the novices were about, speaking only when necessary, and keeping words to a minimum.

"A cup of tea, Sister?" Sister Kate's black veil, flecked with flour, had been tied back, as it always was when she worked in the kitchen, and she wore a blue apron over her black habit. Her sleeves were rolled up to the elbow.

Sister Martha gave a quick look at the back of the novice who stood stirring the pot. Sister Kate followed her glance and spoke louder, in a distinct voice. "Reverend Mother said I might offer you a cup of tea."

"Thank you, Sister."

"Or perhaps a glass of ginger ale. With a straw. That might be easier for you." Again, she glanced back at the novice. "Reverend Mother thought this might be better for you."

Sister Martha nodded. The freezing was beginning to dissipate, but she still held her mouth to one side, trying to make herself look pitiable, as though she were bearing the pain in patience and forbearance for the love of God. She always felt self-conscious around the novices. They generally lived in their own little world upstairs, but there were times like now when proximity was unavoidable. Trying to be models of perfection was a constant burden, impossible to sustain. Among other things, it was hypocritical—as now, when she knew very well that Reverend Mother had said nothing whatsoever to Sister

Kate about offering her either tea or ginger ale, which was kept only for major feast days and cases of stomach flu.

"Here you are, Sister," Sister Kate whispered, handing her a tall glass with a straw. She wondered, watching the bubbles rise to the surface, how long it had been since she'd drunk a glass of ginger ale. Last Christmas probably. A momentary panic seized her. Where would she go to drink it? The nuns' refectory was not possible, in case one of the older nuns, snooping around with nothing else to do, might spot her and run off to tell Reverend Mother.

Sister Kate, sensing her dilemma, shot a quick glance at the novice's back and pointed to the pantry across from the kitchen.

In the pantry, Sister Martha sat and sipped her ginger ale. Her cheek now felt suspended in a strange world between feeling and non-feeling. More than a separate piece of meat, but not quite part of her own mouth. An oilcloth with flowers and watering cans in repetitive patterns covered the small table before her. It looked cheery, almost like a tablecloth that might be in any one of the houses she had passed a while ago. The shelves against the wall, however, told a different story. Food for forty or fifty people per meal: a bin of flour, huge cans labelled "Pears" and "Peaches" and "Plums." A large jar of pickles. Sacks of vegetables on the floor. The small window, looking out onto a scraggly bush, was curtainless.

Sister Kate poked her head in. "Does the ginger ale help, Sister? Or would a cup of tea be better?"

"For God's sake, would you be quiet! It's fine."

She sipped the last of the ginger ale and again looked at her watch. Just past five. She had almost twenty-five minutes before the bell for the evening reading. Perhaps she should report in to Reverend Mother, let her know she had returned. In fact, perhaps she should have reported in as soon as she arrived. Had she been sneaky by coming in the back door, like some silent interloper? She went out so seldom—two years ago was the last time, to get her eyes checked—that she couldn't quite remember the protocol for returning. Yes, perhaps it might be better, just to make sure, to check in with Reverend Mother. Would she be chided for coming in the back way? Reverend Mother was already suspicious of Sister Kate. Sister Martha didn't want herself added to the list of suspects. Life was easier, though no bed of roses, to be sure, if she stayed more or less on the superior's good side.

She started up the back stairs. At the first floor, she walked along the well-polished corridor to the office. This was the part of the convent that visitors saw: the chapel at the end of the corridor and the parlours to one side, lovely old paintings lining the walls, and, on the landing of the magnificent filigreed staircase, a statue of Our Lady of Good Counsel beaming down with a beneficent smile. At rare times, she had the queenly feeling of being inside a stately mansion when she was in this part of the building. Usually, as now, she felt a knot of dread. Her head throbbed. She hoped Reverend Mother would be busy with someone else.

The door of Reverend Mother's office was ajar, and Sister Martha saw that she was alone at her desk. She knocked and entered. "Mother?"

Reverend Mother looked up, her face like a leather purse, set with brown wrinkles. Her veil hung over her arms, and her shoulders were hunched over some papers. She straightened and placed her big hands on her lap. Sister Martha approached the desk and bowed. The pain in her mouth made her feel more vulnerable than usual, and she immediately wished she hadn't come. Reverend Mother might have forgotten that she'd gone out. It was always best to avoid this office entirely if possible.

"Mother, I've just come back from the dentist." She did her best to slur the words.

Reverend Mother lifted her eyebrows, and her hooded eyes widened. "Just come back? I didn't hear the doorbell ring."

"J.J. dropped me off at the back door, Mother." She tried to keep her mouth to the side of her face, downturned and droopy.

"J.J.? Oh yes, Jennifer. The girl with the car. Call people by their proper names, Sister."

"Yes, Mother." The knot tightened inside. She gave a silent burp and felt the lingering bubbles of the ginger ale. Useless to remind herself now that she had not received permission for the drink.

Reverend Mother looked down at her desk, where the newspaper was spread out. "That girl seems a solid, pious sort. She would make a good nun. Of course, her family is well off, and there may be many things that will tempt her to live a life in the world. Still, the grace of God knows no bounds. He may be leading her in the way of a vocation." She opened a desk drawer, took out a pamphlet, and handed it to Sister Martha. "Consider speaking to her. You have my permission. You do teach her, don't you?"

"Yes, Mother. Latin." The cover of the pamphlet was red, with the title in black letters, *Recruiting for Christ.* She felt ridiculous with her face deliberately distorted.

"Latin is the perfect entrée into a talk on religious vocation. The language of the Church, the most pure vehicle for prayer. She's a clever enough girl, is she? Has good grades?"

"She does her best, Mother." How could she begin to tell Reverend Mother that the Latin class had more to do with Julius Caesar's conquest of barbarian Europe than with prayer? That she used the familiar Mass phrases, like *in illo tempore*, as mere examples of grammatical forms? That poor J.J. was hopeless when it came to Latin?

Reverend Mother bent over the newspaper, and Sister Martha remembered the news on the car radio. "Mother, how is the Holy Father?"

"We must pray." She remained fixed on the newspaper. "That will be all, Sister."

Sister Martha hesitated. "Mother, do you think I might go to bed early tonight?" She slurred the words even more deliberately than before.

Reverend Mother looked up and narrowed her eyes. "Whatever for? A bit of drilling on a tooth? Get away with you and put up with it."

Sister Martha slept in fits. Whenever she woke during the night, the unfamiliar feeling of bulk and dull pain inside her mouth gave her the jarring sense that she was another person entirely. When the five-thirty bell roused her the next morning, she was fleetingly aware of a dream in which a faceless man had approached her as she lay prostrate, her black shoes poking up in front of her. He held a band of cloth and began to wrap it tightly around her, beginning at her neck, choking her so that she could barely swallow. A hand clamped her lips shut and the band was pulled over her mouth and wound around her eyes so that she could no longer see. When the band came over the tip of her nose and covered her nostrils, she began to flail and tried to cry out, but she could make no sound because of the muzzle over her mouth.

Morning prayers and Mass were a fog of dissatisfaction and disgust. She still felt a band over her mouth and stretched her lips to answer the prayers. It was a relief to feel her limbs move as she walked out of the chapel and down the stairs.

When breakfast was over, Reverend Mother broke into the silence. She held up the front page of the morning's newspaper. The headline was black and thick: "DEATH OF A POPE." Underneath was a photograph of the Holy Father on a narrow bed, dressed in a nightshirt, eyes closed, his familiar Roman nose in profile, his forearms bare and emaciated. His hands clasped a rosary. Lined up beside him stood a bearded cardinal and an assortment of other men, gazing down at him. The shock of the picture almost overtook the shock of the death itself. The pope in bed: Did they actually allow someone to take such a photograph? The Vicar of Christ, a living saint, he who held the Church together, was now a lifeless body lying upon a narrow bed, his neck exposed, the whole world gawking at him.

In the common room after breakfast, it was difficult to concentrate on planning the day ahead with its review tests and new chapters. Sister Martha opened her desk to find the pamphlet *Recruiting for Christ* that Reverend Mother had given her yesterday. What on earth was she supposed to do with it? She flipped through the pages. "Girls who read frivolous books and movie magazines, who spend time at the movies and watching television are perhaps not likely candidates for the novitiate," the pamphlet said. Then what modern girl would possibly be suitable? Would J.J.? She flipped through more pages—"Modesty in a girl is what you look for"—and slipped the pamphlet back into her desk and gathered up her books and briefcase.

She was glad to escape the gloom cast upon the convent when she crossed the lawn to the school and greeted the girls. Despite the news of the pope's death, they were full of chatter and nonsense. "J.J. better not get extra marks, Sister," one of them said before the last period of the morning began. J.J. smiled. Had the girl talked to the others about yesterday's trip? Did she not know enough to be discreet when chauffeuring the nuns? Sister Martha frowned. That was the last thing she needed this morning—to imagine that the roomful of girls before her had known she'd come away from the dentist's looking like a bloated pig.

Just as she was closing the classroom door, Gwen slid inside. "Oops. Hi, Sister. How's your tooth?" Textbooks and a loose-leaf binder spilled out from her arms. Breathless, her metallic hair tousled, her eyes puffy as if she had just awakened, she rushed across the room to the far row by the windows. Every girl in the school knew what it meant to arrive at the closed door of Sister Martha's classroom: automatic detention. Sister Martha showed no mercy as far as lateness was concerned.

She kept a serious face as she watched Gwen make her bouncy way to her desk, greeting this one and that one.

The queen and her courtiers. Then, she made the sign of the cross: "*In nomine Patris et Filii et Spiritus Sancti.*" The girls shuffled to their feet. "We will pray especially for the repose of the soul of our Holy Father today. And we will ask him to intercede for our Church as well, that God may guide her...." Her voice trailed off. It was so easy to slide into pious talk, into words that meant nothing to the young things in front of her, and that, truth to tell, meant little to her either. Who was she to ask the pope to intercede for anything? What did she know about God's guidance? Rome, the Vatican, St. Peter's Basilica—although the very centre of earthly holiness, they were worlds and worlds away. To be honest, she had to admit that she was more at home with the girls' banter. "*In nomine Patris et Filii et Spiritus Sancti,*" she finished off, relieved that that particular business was now over with.

Papers rustled as the students opened their binders and texts. A roomful of thirty-odd girls, some wearing the cream and maroon cardigan on top of their uniforms, others wearing simply the maroon uniform itself, often reminded Sister Martha of a checkerboard. She liked the cardigans, but they got dirty easily, and on some of the more unkempt of the girls, they had a grey, sloppy look. The cuffs were often stained. At the end of last year, one of the teachers had suggested getting rid of the cream cardigans, but Sister Beatrice said that a roomful of solid maroon would look like a sea of blood. That remark had stopped further discussion.

The girls were more subdued than usual in this late-morning class. Gwen, in spite of her usual fidgetiness, looked oddly dishevelled, her hair uncombed. Right in front of her, J.J. looked bright as a spark, every hair in perfect place.

Sister Martha picked up her textbook from her desk and threw her veil back over her shoulder. "Turn to page one hundred and sixteen, please, to the story of the Sabine women." She ran her hand along the side of her face. The swelling had gone.

"Sister," one of the girls in the front said, "what happens now that the pope is dead?"

Sister Martha was on the verge of answering something like, "This is not the time for such discussion," but she stopped herself. Perhaps, after all, this was an opportunity to discuss the Church and the election of a new pope. These girls had known only one Holy Father, and he had been so saintly and otherworldly as to give the impression that he would live forever. He always wore his all-white garb and was rarely pictured smiling, such was the care of the world upon his shoulders.

"The Holy Father will lie in state at St. Peter's Basilica, and there'll be a funeral Mass, and all the cardinals in the world will assemble in Rome. They'll pray together in the Sistine Chapel until the Holy Ghost inspires them...." She paused, recalling the pope in his nightshirt on his narrow bed. The bearded cardinal looking down at him. "Until then, there's a cardinal who looks after things. I believe he is called the camerlengo."

Some of the girls had begun to fidget. Others were looking out the window or staring into space. No one cared what a camerlengo was. J.J. held her chin in her hand, her elbow on the desk. On the other side of the room, Gwen was chipping away at the nail polish on her thumb. Sister Martha remembered the pope's bony hands clutching a rosary. The wisps of hair rising from his head.

"We won't see his like again," she said. How stupidly pompous. She should at least say something heartfelt. "His Holiness died holding a rosary. Just a simple black rosary, like the one my father used to carry." There was a catch in her throat and, at the same time, she felt a shock inside. The nuns were never to speak of their families. Ever. What on earth had possessed her? She ran her tongue along her back teeth. They felt as smooth as polished marble, almost normal again. She made her voice brisk. "The story of the Sabine women."

In front of her, the rows of girls turned the pages of their textbooks. Legs crossed and uncrossed.

"Of course, you can all tell me the story of the Sabine women," she said, looking around with a small smile. Normally, the girls would have groaned, knowing she was joking because the story in front of them was written in Latin and they'd need help reading it. Today, they stared back with little reaction. "You're like bumps on a log, the lot of you." She felt embarrassed at the way her remark had fallen limp. "Let me tell you then about the Sabine women. Who was the first ruler of Rome?"

"Romulus," a girl whispered from a side row.

"Romulus," Sister Martha repeated. "Now, Rome became a thriving city, but the population stagnated because there were no more children being born. Rome was overpopulated with men and there weren't enough women." She noticed some of the girls exchanging glances and smiles, J.J. among them. She felt herself reddening and wondered if perhaps she should have passed over this story, rushed through third declension adjectives and moved on to the next chapter. But it was too late now. Gwen, she noticed, was looking at her with dark eyes full of attention. The sleepiness had somehow vanished.

"So the Romans hatched a plan. They put on a great festival in honour of the god Neptune and invited all the neighbouring tribes. They wanted, you see, to build a great city and they needed a population. Among the tribes were the Sabines. The Sabine women were very beautiful...." She wanted to stop right there. She remembered a book with a painting of the Sabine women, all white flesh and sensual garments and flowing hair. The book was in the convent library, and the next time she had gone to look for it, it had disappeared.

The class was still, all eyes upon her. She picked up the rosary hanging at her side. The smooth beads felt comforting in her fingers. "So, in the middle of the festivities, the Roman men grabbed the Sabine women and carried them off. They married them and children were born and..."

She held up her hands as if to say, "That's all," when Gwen said in a low voice, "And they all lived happily ever after." Nervous giggles sounded around the room.

"Not quite." It was best to ignore the laughter and barge ahead with the redemptive part of the story. "There came a time when the Romans went to war with the Sabines, but the women begged them to make peace. They couldn't bear to think that their brothers and fathers in their homeland would be making war with their husbands and sons in Rome. And so the Romans made peace with the Sabines."

"Who won?" Gwen again, over in the far row.

"Nobody won, and everybody won. That's how it is when you make peace."

Gwen was leaning forward. Sister Martha pulled out her watch.

"Except that…" Gwen began.

"Look at the time! And we still have to do third declension adjectives!"

The bell rang at the end of the class, and the girls gathered up their books and rushed out in a flurry, as they always did at lunchtime. J.J. gave Sister Martha a friendly wave and a smile before turning away, and then, just like that, she was alone in the cavernous classroom. She looked up to see Gwen standing in the doorway, clutching her bundle of books close to her chest. The dark centres of her eyes stared straight at Sister Martha.

"Sister, what happened to Sister Zélie?"

"Weren't you in her class? She collapsed. That's all I know."

"What's wrong with her?"

"She's in the hospital." The nuns, of course, had been told nothing about Sister Zélie's collapse the day before yesterday.

"Why was her head shaved?"

Sister Martha frowned.

"We let God and the doctors look after Sister Zélie, and we carry on with our own duty."

"They were raped, weren't they, Sister?'

"Who are you talking about?"

"The Sabine women."

She didn't know what to say. The story was written in *Latin*, for heaven's sake. She could have skipped over it and the girls wouldn't have known the difference. Why did she have put her foot in it, only to make herself look foolish? The nuns weren't to broach sexual questions with the girls. This was a subject best left to retreat priests, who spoke to them about the perils of "going steady," and who counselled them in confession. She began to gather up her books. Those two staring eyes, all darkness, were too close. "The point of the story was to illustrate how history develops." She tried speaking brusquely, as if she had better things to do, avoiding eye contact with the girl. "This group of people happens to have power over that group of people, and if that group happens to be in the way, then they get walked over or…"

"Or raped, I guess." Gwen's face was pinched and intense.

"We do need to learn something about the ancient Romans because that is what makes the language come alive. We also want to learn the grammatical rules of the language because that's what's on the exam." She was sputtering nonsense. She was desperate for another nun to come in and rescue her. The church bell began to ring the noon Angelus.

"I should be in chapel now, Gwen." She looked down the length of the room. At the end of one of the rows, a school cardigan was draped over the back of a chair. She walked along the row to retrieve it. Her habit swished and the rosary at her side clattered as she swept down between the desks. Knowing that Gwen was staring after her, she felt like the broadside of a ship.

The cream and maroon sweater hung down along the chair's back, forlorn and dirty-looking. She gathered it up by the neck and began to feel inside for a name tag.

"Sister," Gwen said.

She looked up. The girl was standing at the top of the room looking at her, the books and binder gripped in her arms.

"Sister, what do you have to do to become a nun?"

Sister Martha's hand tightened around the neck of the sweater. She remembered the pamphlet, *Recruiting for Christ*. "Girls who read frivolous books and movie magazines...." Sister Martha had confiscated a movie magazine from Gwen just the other day, coming up from behind during study period just as Gwen was furtively turning pages from inside her loose-leaf binder. Her unusual stillness and concentration had aroused Sister Martha's suspicions. "Modesty in a girl is what you look for...." She remembered how her face burned at the last school retreat day when she saw Gwen's hand go up after the retreat priest had given his "going steady" talk. Gwen had actually asked the silly question, "What if you're in love with the guy, Father?"

"Child," Sister Martha began now. She had hated this form of address herself as a girl, and she hated herself for using it now. "Gwen." She had no idea what to say. From somewhere, a line from *The Song of Bernadette* came back to her. "Our Lord has said, 'I cannot make you happy in this world.'" In fact, Our Lord hadn't said that at all. He said He would give you a hundredfold if you left all to follow Him. This passage was the one used to prove the immense value of the religious life. And yet, she had to admit, "I cannot make you happy in this world," seemed more true to life.

"A nun's way of life is not an easy one," she continued. She felt more herself now. "In fact, it's downright difficult."

Gwen stood rigid. "I know you have to wear those clothes, and you have to pray a lot, and stay in the convent, but..."

"And we have to put up with the likes of you." The Angelus bell was pealing furiously now, and if she was late for prayers again, she would certainly be reprimanded. She could already hear Reverend Mother's gravelly voice telling her that she was on the slippery slope to mediocrity.

Before she could say more, the girl turned and ran out of the classroom. "Gwen," she called. The girl's footsteps faded. The Angelus bell came to an end, and the final peal hung in the air.

4. A Thief in the Night

THE DAY AFTER THE HOLY FATHER, Pope Pius XII, died, Father Doyle drove from his parish across the city to hear the nuns' confessions. The weather was balmy for October, and he had the window rolled down with his elbow out and his left hand resting easy on the wheel. He had thrown a cassock over his black shirt and pants, fastening only two buttons at his waist, and the heavy skirt hung like a limp flap on either side of his feet. As he stopped for a red light, he drummed his fingers along the steering wheel and adjusted the radio dial, switching from a frenetic piece of music to a talk program.

"'Eugenio, are you dead?'" It was the bishop's voice coming out of the speaker. Father Doyle turned up the volume and straightened in his seat, pulling in his arm. "That's the time-honoured question when a pope dies," the bishop continued. "In former times, a silver hammer would be used to strike him on the forehead to confirm his death, but this, of course, isn't done anymore. 'Eugenio' was this pope's original name. If there's no response from him, then the pope is declared dead." The bishop was matter-of-fact, as if reciting the day's sports scores. Father Doyle passed his hand over the back of his neck where the hair had grown in scraggly disorder.

"You mean a doctor doesn't declare the pope dead?" The radio interviewer sounded skeptical.

"Oh, I'm sure the papal doctor was present. But a lot of those ancient rituals are still maintained. Popes go back nearly two thousand years, you know." The bishop's voice was now light and jovial, as if to placate his interviewer. "For example, the pope wears the 'fisherman's ring,' named after St. Peter, who was a fisherman. At the pope's death, the fisherman's ring is taken off his finger and broken. Smashed."

The priest reached down with one hand to fasten the lower buttons of his cassock.

"Then they go off and decide who the next pope will be?" The interviewer seemed to have made the shift from skepticism to a tired cynicism. "But no. First, they have to bury this one."

"Bastard," Father Doyle muttered to the car radio.

"Yes. There's a period of mourning, and of course, the funeral." The bishop seemed to be attempting an even tone.

Father Doyle came to another red light and looked down at the envelope on the seat beside him. It was addressed to him in a neat script. Every letter was perfectly formed, and the address lines on the envelope were straight, as if the writer had used a ruler or a line guide. There was no return address.

The light changed, and he started the car forward again.

"And is a pope embalmed like ordinary mortals?" Another cynical question.

Father Doyle sighed in disgust, and as he reached for the radio dial, he heard the bishop say, "That's another ancient ritual. Herbs come from the Holy Land...." He switched off the radio.

The priest cruised to a stop, letting the car idle in front of St. Monica's Girls' School. He looked over at the red brick front of the building and its two storeys of evenly spaced windows showing no sign of the people inside. He smiled at the sight of a single car, a yellow convertible, parked at the side of the building. He took the letter from the envelope, unfolded it, and read it again. It was written with the same precise penmanship as the writing on the envelope.

Dear Father Doyle,
I know that you are coming to our convent on Friday
as the extraordinary confessor. I want you to know
that I will not be going to confession, but I must speak
with you. One of our senior students gave me a stamp
and is mailing this letter.

It's becoming intolerable here. I'm having trouble
trying to keep St. Monica's together because of the
roadblocks Reverend Mother puts in the way. She
refuses to let me have charge of the finances, so the
heating bill isn't getting paid, and there's no money for
the janitor's salary. That's not everything. One of our
nuns collapsed in the classroom—

The school door burst open and teenage girls poured out, all clad in the maroon uniform, some wearing jackets and others the cream and maroon cardigan. He watched as a small group, led by a girl with short blonde hair, detached itself and headed for the yellow convertible. He looked at his watch, returned the letter to the envelope, and started up the engine. The car turned the corner, cruising alongside the black iron fence, and stopped at the gate in front of the convent's main door.

The convent's electric bell sounded upstairs. Sister Clementia appeared at the pantry door, across from the kitchen. Sister Kate and Sister Martha looked up from where they were sitting at the table. Sister Martha's eyes widened.

"Don't mind Clemmie, Martha," Sister Kate said. "Close the door, Clemmie."

"I don't mind her at all. It's just that I'm still jumpy from the dentist and my talk with Reverend Mother on Wednesday. And I didn't sleep well last night."

"That's the bell," Sister Clementia said. "It's the extraordinary confessor today. We should get up there."

"There's no rush," Sister Martha said. "A fat lot of good the extraordinary confessor does anyway. Coming just four times a year. Things go on the way they always have."

"Was it bad with Zelly, Martha?" Sister Clementia blinked hard through her thick spectacles.

"Don't know. She collapsed, and I assume she was taken to the hospital. Do you think Reverend Mother tells me what's going on? I'm in the doghouse." She stopped and stuck her index finger into the air. "Correction. The dog gets better treatment than any of us do. With the exception of poor old Antonetta, I suppose." She gave a slightly crooked smile. "If we think the extraordinary confessor is going to change things, we've got another thing coming."

"Martha, don't be so…" Sister Kate began.

Sister Martha jumped to her feet. "I have to get out of here. Antonetta may come along. Then it'll be the telegraph wire. Aunty Tony to Reverend Mother. Straight through, without delay." With a flurry of skirt and rosary beads she headed for the door.

"Wait!" Sister Clementia called. She pulled a folded cloth from her pocket. It was the runner she had been carrying around ever since she had taken it from Sister Zélie's desk. "You do lovely embroidery. Can you fix this?"

Sister Martha took the cloth and held it out in front of her. "This is a beautiful piece. Where have I seen it before?"

"On the table in the library," Sister Clementia said. "It needs fixing along the edge."

"I see." She fingered the scorched edging. "This will keep my mind off other things." She put the cloth in her pocket and left the pantry.

Upstairs in the chapel, Sister Martha knelt down in the confession line at the back. The young nun beside her, Sister Julianne, lifted her eyebrows, and inclined her head to the confessional. Inside, one of the nuns was speaking in a low, agitated voice. Sister Martha clenched her hands together. The other nun put her finger to her lips and faced the altar and tabernacle, picking up the rosary hanging from her belt. Sister Martha pulled from her pocket her permissions book and turned to the page on which she had written "Confessions." Underneath, she had scribbled a series of words: "silence," "obedience," "charity to girls." She wrote "disrespect," then put the book back in her pocket.

The priest's side of the confessional was dark except for a small window that showed a hint of sky. The brick wall of St. Monica's Girls' School rose beyond the hedge. Father Doyle sat with a purple stole around his neck. He rested his head against the back of the chair and ran a finger around the inside edge of his Roman collar. He then leaned over to the dark screen, his chin in his hands.

On the other side of the confessional screen, Sister Beatrice knelt in darkness. The only thing visible to her was the outline of the priest's head.

"I have a vow of obedience, Father, but I've come to a point where it's no longer possible," she whispered. "She's taken obedience to the extreme and has a poor old demented nun spying on me. The Holy Rule no longer means anything."

"Do you think you have obligations that go beyond your vow of obedience?" Father Doyle whispered.

"Yes, but how do I meet those obligations?"

The priest was silent.

Sister Beatrice continued: "I'm asking you for help, Father. Where else can I go?"

"I'll speak to the bishop, if you like. But you must give me permission. As you know, anything said in confession...."

The following Monday morning, Sister Beatrice stood in the principal's office beside the desk, which was piled with papers and file folders. "She sent Aunty Tony over here with a jug of water," she whispered. Sister Martha stood across from her and looked back at the door every few minutes.

"She's even tormenting her favourite spy now," the principal continued. "Forcing the poor old dear to carry a full jug of water all the way over here. Aunty Tony presented me with the jug a few minutes ago and said, 'Reverend Mother says that all the nuns are to have a drink of water at ten o'clock.'"

"So she can see who's talking to whom," Sister Martha said.

"The school will become a circus, and I'll be responsible. She's setting me up for a fall."

Sister Martha went to the door and looked out. Sister Antonetta was strolling to the far end of the corridor. "Aunty Tony's gone for a walk. What did you say to Father Doyle on Friday?"

"Oh, what does it matter? He told me he'd speak to the bishop. But nothing will change."

The bell rang for the homeroom period. Sister Martha started. "I didn't realize it was that time. I must dash."

In the doorway, she made way for Sister Antonetta to enter, and then rushed away.

"I'm to stay in here until the drink at ten o'clock," Sister Antonetta said. "Reverend Mother said so. I must have some glasses."

"We have no glasses in the school. Just one or two in case of an emergency. If someone needs to take medicine." Sister Beatrice sat down at her desk, opened a file, and picked up a pen.

Sister Antonetta stood looking at her. "What else do you keep in case of an emergency?"

Sister Beatrice looked up. "What do you mean?"

"Do you keep sweets? Cookies?"

The principal put her pen down. "If Reverend Mother said the nuns were all to come here for a drink of water at ten o'clock, they will. But they'll need glasses, unless you want them to drink directly from the jug. If you'd brought the empty jug and filled it here, you could have carried glasses at the same time. But I know Reverend Mother told you to fill the jug with water first and bring it over. You practised holy obedience even though it didn't make sense. Anyway, we don't have glasses here, and I have my work to do."

"Yes, but do you keep cookies for an emergency? Or candy? For people with diabetes you need candy at hand, you know."

Sister Beatrice sat back and looked up at the ceiling. Her cheeks had turned pink. "Sister, we don't keep cookies or candy. We have no diabetic girls in the school. If you have diabetes, you must speak to Reverend Mother."

"Oh, she wouldn't bother herself with..." Sister Antonetta snapped her mouth closed.

Sister Beatrice took a breath. "I'm reluctant to take students out of class, but I will get a couple of girls to go with you to the convent to bring over some glasses. Wait here."

She got up and left the office with a swish of her habit against the door frame. Sister Antonetta watched her leave and then tiptoed to a cupboard at the side of Sister Beatrice's desk. She inched open the latch and looked inside. Stacks of coil notebooks filled the top shelf. On the middle shelf were two glasses and a white first-aid kit. She pulled down the kit and opened it. There was a small bottle of iodine, a gauze bandage roll, a small pair of scissors, a box of Band-Aids in individual wrappers. She opened the box and slipped out a Band-Aid. She fingered the red string at the side of it and began to tug. Just then, Sister Beatrice returned with two girls behind her.

Sister Antonetta jumped, thrust the Band-Aid into her pocket and stood fumbling with the first-aid kit. The two nuns looked at each other in silence, and the girls stared from one to the other. Then the principal said in an even voice, "Here are J.J. and Sally, Sister. They mustn't take too much time from their chemistry class. Please go over to the convent with them now and get the glasses." She held out her hand and took the first-aid kit. "Thank you, Sister. This comes in handy in an emergency."

The nun led the way along the path to the convent, the two girls following behind. Nearing the back door, she turned to them. "I don't suppose you have any sweets in your lunch."

The girls looked at each other. "Sweets, Sister?" Sally said.

"I have this extra duty now. Taking water to the nuns in the school. On top of everything else I have to do. Sweets give a person extra energy." When they reached the back door, she said, "You must wait here. This is the cloister. It's specially consecrated. Just as *we're* specially consecrated. Now, just wait here."

The girls leaned against the railing that led to the door and gave each other puzzled looks.

Inside, Sister Antonetta hastened up the back stairs to Reverend Mother's office. As she reached the door, the superior opened it. She took hold of Sister Antonetta's habit skirt and pulled her into the office. "What is it?"

"Mother, Sister Martha was in Sister Beatrice's office." Sister Antonetta stood still, her hands clasped.

Reverend Mother let go of her skirt. "Yes?"

"And they were speaking."

"What were they saying? Were they breaking charity?"

"Yes, I'm sure, Mother. That is to say, I'm not *sure*, but..."

"I asked you to stay there until the nuns have their drink of water at ten o'clock. That was an order of obedience."

"Mother, I'm sorry, but all I could manage was to carry the water in the big white jug from the refectory. I had to come back for glasses."

"And who gave you permission to use that jug?"

"I presumed permission, Mother. It was the only way I could get water over to the school."

"That jug has one purpose only, and that is to carry water for the refectory washing-up. We do not use things for any reason other than their originally intended purpose. This is a mark of holy poverty as well as religious obedience. You should have asked for a jug in the kitchen."

"I didn't have permission, Mother."

"Well, be off with you, then. You and your disobedience."

Reverend Mother turned away. Sister Antonetta bowed and said, "Mother, there are no glasses at the school to drink the water."

"You should have thought of that in the first place," the superior said, her back to the other nun.

"Mother, Sister Beatrice said I should have got the water from the school instead of lugging it over from the convent. I told her that I was doing what you told me to do."

"That nun knows nothing of obedience," Reverend Mother said.

"What should I tell the girls, Mother?"

"Girls?"

"Sister Beatrice sent two of them with me to get some glasses."

Reverend Mother turned, suddenly alert. "Where are these girls?"

"They're outside the back door, Mother." Sister Antonetta shifted from one foot to the other and tightened her hand clasp.

"Why have you kept them waiting?" Reverend Mother bustled her out the door and followed her into the corridor.

When Sister Antonetta appeared at the back door a few moments later, she held a tray of glasses in shaking hands. Reverend Mother, right behind her, carried another. They gave the trays to each of the girls.

Reverend Mother's face was gentle as she surveyed them. "And what are your names?"

"Jennifer Jones, Reverend Mother," J.J. said, blushing under the nun's scrutiny. She balanced the tray of glasses between two hands.

"Ah yes, the girl with the car. And you?"

"Sally Sullivan, Reverend Mother."

"Alliteration. J.J. and S.S. You know what 'alliteration' means, of course." She gave a slight smile, and her wrinkles deepened.

"Yes, Reverend Mother," Sally said. She shifted her tray.

"You must be Dr. Sullivan's daughter. He's a good doctor. I remember when one of our sisters had terrible breath. You couldn't stand to be near her. Your father discovered the cause—it was her adenoids! I had never known that adenoids could be the cause of bad breath. They were infected." She paused, as if to let the information sink in. "Once he removed them, her breath was fine. And when I was weak and sick, it was Dr. Sullivan who said, undulant fever. The milk wasn't sufficiently pasteurized, you see. My gallbladder...." She stood awkwardly, as if unsure of what to say next.

Sally smiled with shyness and embarrassment.

"And are you both doing well in your studies?"

The girls nodded. "Yes, Reverend Mother," J.J. said.

"Off with you, then."

The trio made its way back to the school, each girl carrying a tray, with Sister Antonetta following behind.

"It comes to everyone, death does," Lizzie said. "No man is let off. That's what Father said at Mass yesterday." She stood folding towels and face cloths in front of the laundry window. "A lovely sermon it was, all about the Holy Father. He's to be buried today." She paused and half-turned to Sister Clementia, who was drying her hands after setting some white garments into a tub to soak. "Frank looking at his watch the whole time during the sermon and not hearing a word," she continued.

She brushed a wisp of greying hair from her forehead and turned completely. "I say to him—in a whisper—I say, 'Would you listen to him for once? He's talking about the Holy Father.' And he says back to me, 'That one likes the sound of his own voice.'" She resumed her work. "Was it blasphemy, Sister? Is that what he committed?"

"I don't know, I'm..." Sister Clementia began.

"Is it blasphemy to speak ill of the priests?" Lizzie stood still and stared out the window. "Glory be to God, would you look at this, Sister? The virgin martyrs off to their deaths. Is that not what it looks like?"

Sister Clementia came over beside her and looked out the

window. Two St. Monica's girls and Sister Antonetta had emerged from the convent's back door and were walking in single file on the path to the school, the girls carrying trays of drinking glasses. The nun followed, waving her arms as if shooing them forward.

"Or is it lambs to the slaughter, Sister?"

"What's the woman up to?" Sister Clementia murmured.

They watched the procession until the three disappeared behind the hedge. Sister Clementia went back to the tub and began to scrub.

"The photograph of him in the newspaper, Sister. Lying in his bed in his nightshirt. Did you see it?"

"Yes, Lizzie. But I didn't see it plain. Reverend Mother only held it up for a second."

"Why did they photograph him like that? I thought of me mother's wake, Sister." Lizzie shook her head. "We'd never think of taking a photograph of her in her nightdress, all soaked as it was, and we'd never let anyone see her like that. We washed her all over and put on her best dress, blue it was, like her eyes, though we couldn't see them anymore because of them being closed, God rest her soul." Lizzie made the sign of the cross. "There was a ruffle at the neck that hid the scrawniness of it, and we brushed her hair back and fixed it in a bun. This was before we ever let Mr. Leary in, the funeral man. Should they not have done that for the Holy Father, Sister? Dressed him up properly before taking the pictures?"

"Yes, you'd think so." Sister Clementia spoke absently as she rubbed her red knuckles.

"Father said yesterday we must wait for the watchman. The watchman in the night."

"Yes, it's a psalm from the Bible, Lizzie. As the watchman waits for daylight, we must wait for the Lord. We say these prayers when one of the nuns dies. The day of your death, it's like a thief in the night."

"'Like a thief in the night.' Yes, that's it. Father said that too. It's a terrible thought—a thief coming in and stealing from you when you're asleep. Do you think he was robbed, Sister? Is that why he thought of it?"

"No, it's from the Bible too, Lizzie. Saint Paul in one of his epistles."

"Is that a fact, Sister? But isn't it true." She looked at the nun. "Fancy me saying something in the Bible is true," and the two began to laugh.

"Passing judgment on the Bible." Sister Clementia passed her hand over her eyes.

"But Sister, isn't it so that if death comes on you like a thief, you must be ready?" Lizzie took a stack of towels from the table and placed them on a shelf.

"I should say so, Lizzie. Ready at all times."

"Now poor old Sister Antonetta—why d'you think the three of them marched over to the school like that? Her and the two girls?"

"It's Reverend Mother's feast day the day after tomorrow. Maybe they're getting ready for it."

"Sister Antonetta's in charge now?" Lizzie looked back at Sister Clementia from the corner of her eye.

"She's keeping an eye on the nuns in the school. Making sure they don't speak. Because of the rule of silence. I think that's it. She's Reverend Mother's eyes."

"But the nuns is teachers, Sister. How can they teach if they're not allowed to speak?"

Sister Clementia shrugged and remained silent.

"Rockets, Your Excellency?" Father Doyle stood before the bishop in his wood-panelled office. The silver-haired bishop sat at an enormous desk with a leather top. He waved the priest to a chair. The purple stone in his ring gleamed.

"Yes, they've been shooting rockets at the moon. It's almost taken over the Holy Father's death on the front pages." The bishop sat forward and fingered his pectoral cross. "Did you hear my radio interview? I was all set to talk about our late Holy Father—the efforts he made toward world peace. His struggle against Communism. And what do I get from the interviewer? What do I know about how a pope is embalmed?"

Father Doyle nodded. "They always want the voyeuristic details."

"But the good man is now gone, God rest his soul, and the race is on among the *papabili*," the bishop continued.

"Have you heard any predictions, Your Excellency?"

"The cardinal archbishop of Bologna is a champion of labour unions. Ruffini has stood up to the Mafia, so they say. There's a man of courage, wouldn't you think? Then there's Cardinal Ottaviani who wants to throw the infidels out of Catholic countries, as if we're back in 1492. But you're not here to discuss the *papabili*."

There was silence between them, and then Father Doyle spoke. "Your Excellency, I told one of the sisters at St. Monica's that I would speak with you about that superior of theirs. She's making impossible demands. It's hard for the school to function properly."

"St. Monica's is an excellent school, from what I hear. Is this just a bitter nun talking? Wanting her own way?"

"Your Excellency, this was the principal. It's the Reverend Mother who..."

"It may be best if I have a word with her. I don't like to meddle when things are going well, but..." He waved a dismissive hand at Father Doyle. The priest remained seated, and the bishop looked up with surprise. "Is there something else?"

"Your Excellency, I wondered if perhaps I could be relieved of the role of extraordinary confessor to those nuns." He folded and unfolded his hands. "I thought I could help out at St. Monica's. As a chaplain, perhaps."

"You'd prefer teenage girls to neurotic nuns and their litanies of little sins, is that it?"

The priest blushed. "I don't know that I'd put it that way."

"We'll see. In the meantime, I'll talk to that Reverend Mother."

During the lull before the last period of the morning, Sister Martha stood by the window of her homeroom as the students entered in chattering groups of two and three. She held up several skeins of embroidery thread in shades of ivory and white. Sally and J.J. sauntered over to her.

"What's that you're doing, Sister?" Sally asked.

She unfolded the wrinkled runner and held it up for the girls to see. "This is an exemplary model of cutwork. You wouldn't believe the patience it takes to cut these tiny holes so that no thread is broken." She let her hand hover over the blue and pink flowers. "It seems hardly possible that a human hand made these perfect stitches."

"Whose is it, Sister?" J.J. asked.

"It doesn't matter. We hold all things in common in the religious life."

The bell rang, and the students scrambled to their seats.

"Em*broider,* ade*noider*," J.J. said in a singsong voice as she walked to her desk.

"You're a poet and don't know it," Sally said.

Sister Martha folded the runner in haste and slipped it with the embroidery threads into her black work-bag. "Attendance," she called. "Texts open to today's chapter: 'The Future Indicative Active.'"

5. The New Girl

SISTER MARTHA NEEDED A NEW GIRL in her first-year Latin class like she needed another hole in her head. Especially this week. Tomorrow was Reverend Mother's feast day, and already giddiness was spreading like jelly throughout the school. The new girl stood before her as she sat at her desk mulling over the attendance register and waiting for class to begin. She said her name was Brooke. Brooke? Sister Martha frowned. What kind of a name was that?

"Are you a running stream?" she asked the girl, making a wave motion with her hand. That was bad enough, but it could have been worse; she had almost said, "Are you a babbling brook?" Something had stopped her, thanks be to God. She managed perhaps ten times a day to make herself look foolish in front of the girls, and each time, the humiliation stung. But it was good for the soul.

"It has an 'e' at the end," the girl said. Her soft voice seemed out of sync with her looks. She had a face of classic beauty—Sister Martha immediately thought of Elizabeth Taylor in *National Velvet*, one of the last movies she had seen before she entered the convent—with a high white forehead and perfectly arched eyebrows and dark hair that curled slightly around her ears. So beautiful she might have been a snob, might have cut short Sister Martha's stupid attempts at humour. She might have stared at her with contempt. Instead, there was a naiveté about the girl, as if she were a child on her first day of kindergarten. Her complexion reminded Sister Martha of a satiny white rose, with the barest of pink on her cheeks. Her speckled eyes gazed with a kind of purity. "A man in whom there is no guile," Jesus had said of Nathaniel, and He might also have said the same thing of this girl. Guilelessness was a virtue that Sister Martha herself tried to cultivate. Without success, it had to be added.

She picked up her pen and regarded the attendance register. She couldn't gawk at the girl all day. "Your last name?"

"Hankey," said the girl.

Sister Martha looked at her again. The perfect face, the long white neck above the maroon school uniform. For some reason, she had expected the girl's last name to be "Du Barry" or "*de la*" something or other.

"Hanky-panky?" she said. *Oh, ha, ha, ha.* Why couldn't she think before she spoke?

"It's spelled H-a-n-k-e-y." The same steady childlike gaze. Sister Martha wanted to melt into the floor.

"Do you have the textbook?" It was an abrupt question, almost querulous-sounding to her own ears, an attempt at distancing herself. She should have addressed the girl by her name, but it felt too alien, like addressing someone as "Horse" or "Meadow" or "Tree."

The girl pulled the brown Latin textbook from the bundle that she held to her chest. "Is this it, Sister?"

Sister Martha stared at the girl. *Sister.* She hadn't expected such deference from this lovely creature in front of her, this child belonging to another realm. It would be more fitting for authority and wisdom to stream out of her mouth, like the Child Jesus in the temple, rather than a simple polite question. But it was too stupid, this mooning over a student. She nodded. "You can find a desk at the back," she said. She stood up and walked to the door. What if the others, who were chattering their way into the classroom, knew how unnerved she was by this new girl?

She waved in the last stragglers, and closed the door with a flourish. The gesture only half-worked. The chattering diminished somewhat, but with the scraping of chairs and the opening of binders and textbooks, the noise level remained much the same. She moved back to the teacher's desk, pushed the sleeves of her habit to halfway up her chubby white forearms, and clapped her hands for attention.

The girls shuffled to their feet. The room seemed awash in colour and vitality. The maroon uniform had been softened by last year's addition of detachable cream-coloured collars. "These collars are hell to iron, Sister," that upstart Gwen had complained at the time.

Sister Martha had recoiled in mock horror at the girl's profanity. "Shut your mouth, girl!" She felt a secret thrill whenever one of them came out with remarks like this. It showed they trusted her and, yes, considered her open-minded enough. One of them, yet still a nun.

"*In nomine Patris et Filii et Spiritus Sancti,*" she said, making the sign of the cross. More shuffling as the girls stopped fiddling with their hair and more or less blessed themselves. With these first-year students, she sometimes stopped in the middle of the prayer to give a lesson on the proper way of making the sign of the cross, but mostly, she just soldiered on. She noticed that Brooke had found the last seat in the far left row. Her prettiness seemed to extend itself in a kind of halo. In comparison, the girls around her looked drab, their hair limp and mousy, their faces bland.

"*Pa-ter Nos-ter qui es in cae-lis...*" Most of the girls looked down at their notebooks, where they had copied the prayer, not yet entirely sure of the words. They heard the "Our Father" in Latin every Sunday at Mass, and the more pious among them nearly every day. But it was one thing to hear the priest mumbling up there at the altar, and another thing entirely to get your own tongue around the words. It was only a month and a half into the term, and still Sister Martha pronounced every syllable slowly. Latin prayers were useful when it came to showing examples of grammatical lessons she was teaching to the first-year students. One could spot the genitive case, for instance, in *Filii*. She often said, "See now, you'll be able to understand the Mass a bit more, and you'll see why word endings change."

When the prayer was over and the girls took their seats, an intelligent, flabby-faced student named Gina put up her hand. "Sister, in Latin, the verb goes at the end of the sentence. But at Mass when the priest says, '*Dominus vobiscum*,' there isn't a verb at all even though it's translated as 'The Lord be with you.' How come?"

"How come what?" She was groping for time. Gina was a cocky child, a bit too big for her britches. Gina could always be counted on to ask questions she didn't have an answer for.

"How come '*Dominus vobiscum*' doesn't have a verb?"

Best to flub an answer. "It would normally be the subjunctive mood because it's a wish or perhaps a blessing: 'May the Lord be with you.'"

"Maybe it just means, 'The Lord with you,' like, 'The Lord *is* with you.' Perhaps it's straight indicative, not subjunctive at all."

Good Lord. Most of the students knew nothing of indicative and subjunctive in first-year Latin. Why couldn't Gina just go off and teach herself?

In the far row, Brooke was adjusting the collar on her brand-new uniform. The whiteness of it made the other girls' collars look yellow and shabby.

"Texts open, please," Sister Martha called. She picked up her own textbook and opened it at the page she had marked with her mother's mortuary card. It was utterly the wrong use for the card, and she made a mental note to remove it and put it in her daily missal or her New Testament, neatly stacked at her spot in the chapel, where she could pray for her mother's soul in peace and recollection. The card's picture of Our Lady of Perpetual Help, with Mary's sorrowful face and tiny adult Jesus sitting in her hand like a ventriloquist's dummy, was not Sister Martha's favourite, not by a long shot. She would have preferred the Madonna della Strada. The likeness of her favourite Madonna had come to her on a Christmas card one year, and she had carefully cut out the picture to use as the main marker in her New Testament. When she felt battered and bruised by Reverend Mother or when she had opened her mouth too often or too indiscreetly with some of the girls, she liked to sit in chapel—just sit there—and look down at the picture of the lovely young Mary in her blue cloak with the rose-mouthed Babe nestled against her shoulder.

She flipped over the mortuary card. "Those who sow in tears shall reap rejoicing. Ellen Mary Cullen, 1900–1950. May she rest in peace." Her mother had died in the Holy Year, eight years ago now, just after the canonization of Maria Goretti. The canonization had been a huge affair. A girl, just slightly younger than the students in front of her, had been declared a saint. The manner of her death brought to mind all the trials and temptations of girls just coming into womanhood. To die defending her chastity against an evil-minded wretch. And then to forgive him! Not only that, but her attacker had had a spectacular conversion while in prison.

She remembered the celebration in the school at the time. The senior girls had carried banners showing St. Maria Goretti carrying an armful of lilies and looking like the ethereal virgin martyrs of the first century rather than a peasant girl from central Italy. But never mind—it had been a memorable occasion, from the palm leaves, the symbol of martyrdom, to the banners showing Maria in a simple white gown, and then to the stirring words of Father Raymond. He had come down the street from Purification Church to preside over the festivities (and, truth be told, he had preened as he strode back and forth on the stage of the assembly hall). Sister Martha had noticed that he seemed to pay particular attention to the pretty girls as he pranced through the school corridors, barely acknowledging the plain ones, or even the nuns. She would have loved to sit down and talk with him about matters of importance, like how to overcome distractions during prayer and learn to pray with greater fervour. But, of course, the nuns were forbidden to talk to anyone without permission, priests included. He never gave her the nod anyway, being enthralled as he was with the pretty girls—the older ones, especially the girls with long dark hair, she noticed. Or perhaps that was just her imagination.

She rocked back and forth from one foot to another in an effort to come back to the present. "All right, has everyone read Chapter Ten?" She tucked her mother's mortuary card between pages further on in the book and smoothed down the centre of the page with her hand. "The Vocative Case," she said. She looked around the class. Most of the girls were still opening their binders and grabbing their texts from the floor. "What's the vocative case? Can anyone tell me?"

Gina raised her hand. "It's when you're going to address somebody."

"Right. *Ave, Maria.* Hail, Mary. *Maria* is in the vocative case because she is being addressed. The angel Gabriel is speaking to her. What do you notice about the ending of the name, *Maria*?" She saw that Brooke was still fumbling through the pages. Her text looked brand new, as if it had never been opened. "Page fifty-five," she called down the far row. "What about the ending?"

A snicker rose from the second row to her right, and she thought she heard a whisper, "What about it?" She ran her finger between the wimple and the soft fold of her chin where perspiration had begun to form. Lightening up was in order. "Hail to the lot of you. Wake up! What is the nominative ending of *Maria*? The nominative?"

"It's 'a,'" she heard from somewhere.

"Yes, 'a,'" she repeated. "And the vocative? Exactly the same. There are some exceptions—masculine nouns of the second declension—but mostly the vocative ending is the same as the nominative." The girls were restive, squirming in their chairs, looking out the window. No wonder. She was bored herself.

"Sister." It was Gina.

Sister Martha felt relieved; Miss Genius might say something helpful for a change. She nodded at her.

"I read the autobiography of Winston Churchill, where he was learning Latin as a kid, and the teacher told him he had to decline *mensa*, which is the word for *table*."

"Yes." Sister Martha could have kissed the girl with gratitude. Let her talk about Winston Churchill forever.

"And when he came to the vocative, he asked what it meant, and the teacher said you use the vocative if you want to address the table. And Churchill said, 'why would I want to talk to a table,' and the teacher threw him out of the class."

Around the room, there were smiles and looks to one another. The sleeping beauties had come back to life. Sister Martha raised her voice, trying to sound jocular. "And why not? The last thing that teacher needed was a smart know-it-all in the class. He was simply trying his best to get Latin through *thick heads.*"

Was it her imagination, or did the air turn dead again? Perspiration began to form on Sister Martha's back. She felt a vague itch somewhere between her shoulder blades. The wood-lined room was an unrelenting brown. Unlike the classrooms in elementary schools, which were cheery with plants and children's artwork, this room displayed nothing except for a black crucifix with its silver-coloured corpus above the blackboard.

In the far row, Brooke leaned over to her neighbour and whispered.

"Anything you want to say, Brooke?"

Brooke looked up, startled. Her face and neck turned splotchy. "No, thank you," she said. Just that—"No, thank you"—as if she were a small child with good manners who had just refused the offer of candy.

Sister Martha readjusted her veil and held her book up again. "Right. Let's take a look at the first and second declensions."

Down the centre row, a girl pointed to something in the book, grabbing her neighbour's attention.

"Anything to say, Marianne?" The girl had long fingernails, the artificial kind that had become a fad with some of the younger girls. She wore her hair in a ponytail.

"Just looking at the picture, Sister. A cockfight." The girls around her tittered. Sister Martha looked down at her text. The picture showed a tile design for a Roman floor, two roosters glaring at one another with beady eyes, their feathers raised. The caption read, "A lively cockfight would always draw an interested audience in Rome." The ones who had laughed were the cheap girls with dyed hair and thin eyebrows plucked in a tarty way. Sister Martha read the caption aloud, drawing a general guffaw this time, even among some of the simple ones, those who normally didn't cause a fuss.

"A lively cockfight," said Sister Martha again, mystified, and this time the whole class broke into a roar. Even the pasty-faced Gina smiled.

"Cock-a-doodle-doooo!" someone called.

Sister Martha drew herself up. A feeling of panic always grabbed her in the chest whenever she felt she was losing control of a class. Try to head it off, to make light of the situation. "Forget the cockfight," she shouted, but the din only grew louder. "Quiz!" she yelled. "*Quiz tomorrow!*"

She wasn't sure how she got through the rest of the class, but when the bell rang and the girls slammed their books shut and clambered to their feet, she turned her back to them and fixed her gaze on the black work-bag she had placed on a shelf by the windows.

Needlework always brought her a sense of calm accomplishment, the needle moving in and out at her direction. She was taking the place of God, in a sense, in creating something beautiful by choosing the thread, deciding on the stitch, using her talent with every pull and snip. There was poetic justice, as well, in that the task had been given to her not by Reverend Mother, who wouldn't trust her to mend a tea towel, but by the most insignificant member of the community, little Sister Clementia.

"Sister, did you know the pope's doctor was a fake?" a voice said behind her.

Sister Martha jumped and turned. Gina was standing before her. Brooke stood a few paces behind. Gina always seemed to have one or two of the less intelligent girls trailing after her like acolytes, but why this beautiful creature, with her silky skin and perfectly coiffed hair? Had Gina importuned her, seeing in her a dull and therefore malleable companion? Or had Brooke cozied up to Gina, knowing her intelligence to be an asset?

"That's ridiculous. The Holy Father had the best of medical attention. The cardinals around him would have seen to that." Gina annoyed her to no end. Sister Martha wanted nothing more than for her and her minion to disappear so that she could dive into her work-bag and pick up the soothing piece of cutwork.

"Oh, no, it's true. They're firing the doctor. He's going to publish a diary of the pope's last days."

Sister Martha remembered the photograph of the late pope in the newspaper, lying in his bed, dying or perhaps already dead, covered with only a sheet, his spindly arms exposed, the collar of his nightshirt open for the world to see.

"My parents get *Il Giorno*. That's an Italian newspaper, and it says that the doctor took the pope's body away and put some awful embalming stuff inside him, and he turned all yellow and started to disintegrate. That's why his funeral was yesterday. Normally it should have been nine days after he died." The girl spoke with eagerness, delighted to be passing on ghoulish details.

"That's enough. You're showing disrespect for the late Holy Father with that kind of talk. You should be ashamed of yourself." Sister Martha felt a malicious smile forming that she was powerless to wipe away. "You think you're smart because you know something about Latin verbs and because your parents get an Italian newspaper. You think you know more about our late Holy Father than we do. You always think you know everything, but do you know what you are? You're just a puffed-up ignoramus, and in fact, you know nothing. I've seen the way you have stupid girls following you so that you can look smart. Girls like…" She gestured at Brooke, her arm shaking.

Gina stood facing her, her pasty face blanched, her unblinking eyes somewhere between defiant and hurt. Behind her, Brooke stared.

When Sister Martha said nothing more, Gina turned and left the classroom, her shoulders squared, Brooke scurrying behind her like a puppy.

Sister Martha sank into her chair. Thank God for an exquisite piece of embroidery to work on. She opened her work-bag and pulled out the runner. Gina and her *Il Giorno*—that girl was surely in need of a dressing down. Better to let her know early in the year that Sister Martha was in charge of this classroom and knew better than she did about the affairs of the Church. But had she, Sister Martha, failed in charity? Was her outburst a matter for confession? And Brooke—what did the new girl now think of her Latin teacher? She tried smoothing out the wrinkles in the cloth. Reverend Mother had, of course, told the nuns nothing about the pope's funeral. As she fingered the cutwork holes, she imagined that the whole thing was disintegrating in her hands.

6. Reverend Mother's Feast Day

SISTER BEATRICE PULLED OUT HER pocket watch. Ten minutes before the next bell. On the rare occasions like right now when she found herself at loose ends, she liked to walk the length of the first floor corridor and stand at the door the girls used, the one facing the street, looking out the window. It was Wednesday, the spine-breaker of the week. It was also Reverend Mother's feast day, and before it was over, there might be more than spines broken. She smiled at the grim joke.

She sometimes wished she could go outside and check on the condition of the steps and sidewalk, the fence and the letters on the building's façade, but that territory belonged to the janitor—and Reverend Mother, of course. So she dared not venture forth; who knew what eyes were watching behind the lace curtains of the houses across the street? An innocent remark from a neighbour to one of the nuns might bring her to her knees in front of the community. Today, though, there were more pressing things. If she wished for anything, it would be to have this afternoon's concert over with.

She didn't linger at the window. Instead, she turned back and stood for a moment before the picture on the corridor wall just inside the door. It was a paint-by-numbers, crudely completed in places, featuring an English cottage with a blue stream, a green meadow, some pink and yellow flowers, and a blue sky with a streak of white clouds. The picture sat inside a thin brown frame. Beside it hung a copper plaque: "Painted by Cathy Maloney, 1941-1958." Cathy was a senior girl who had died in the late spring. Cancer had shown no mercy, taking her cruelly, bit by bit. A few weeks after her death, the girl's mother, a clumsy, inelegant woman with unkempt hair and crookedly applied red lipstick, appeared at the school one day. "Cathy finished this just before she went blind," she said to Sister Beatrice as she drew the picture from a brown grocery bag. "She loved St. Monica's, and you Sisters were so kind to her. It would be nice if a part of her stayed here."

Reverend Mother had consented to having the plaque made. Sister Beatrice felt gratified to see the usually chattering girls often stopping to gaze at the picture, wrapped for a moment in an aura of silence. Except for the new girls, they had all known who Cathy was. She herself was unsure about the cheap frame. Did it speak of the girl's suffering and courage? Or did it make her—and by extension the school and the convent—look cheap in return? Should she ask Reverend Mother for a bolder frame, perhaps matching the plaque? For now, the picture remained as the lumbering Mrs. Maloney had presented it to the school. Returning back along the corridor, she stopped at the open door of Sister Julianne's classroom. The first-year religion lesson inside was intriguing.

"The Orthodox missionaries went to Alaska across the Bering Strait, and they put up with the harshness of the weather, the constant rain, for the love of God. Their long beards and fierce eyes scared the natives. The natives had rings through their noses, so they were pretty scary too." Sister Julianne was holding forth in her little-girl voice. Sister Beatrice peeked through the gap in the doorway. The students within her line of vision had their eyes on the front of the room. Sister Julianne was holding their attention. But what was the point of such a lesson? Well, it didn't matter. No harm in listening to stories about Orthodox missionaries, as long as Reverend Mother didn't find out.

"What propelled them to leave their own comfortable land in Europe and go to the wilds of the Alaskan frontier?" Sister Julianne continued. "The same thing that has driven missionaries all over the world. Zeal to spread the faith to the ends of the earth and the spirit of religious obedience."

Sister Beatrice saw Gina raise her hand. "But the faith of the Orthodox isn't the true faith, is it, Sister?"

Sister Julianne didn't miss a beat. "That's right. The Orthodox are not Catholics. Actually, they're *un*orthodox because they don't believe in the infallibility of the pope, but their sacrifices were just as great as those of Saint Francis Xavier or any of the others. Yes, Gina?"

The girl's hand was raised again. "What about that, Sister? I mean, the pope is dead, and there's no new pope yet. What happens to that infallibility belief?"

Sister Beatrice smiled. Girls like Gina, who thought of conundrums that hadn't occurred to their teachers, were sometimes an annoyance in the classroom, but they often became a feather in the school's cap. Gina was scholarship material.

"When the cardinals elect a new pope, he'll be infallible too," Sister Julianne said. Her voice was as smooth as a calm lake. "In the meantime..."

The school bell sounded in the corridor, and Sister Beatrice jumped. How long had she been standing there? Up and down the corridor, in all the classrooms, teenage girls were getting to their feet with the scraping of desks and the noise of voices letting loose. She stopped at Sister Martha's classroom and looked in. Sister Martha was standing by the window, clutching her work-bag . She looked up in surprise.

"What have I caught you at?" Sister Beatrice meant it as a lighthearted remark, a reprieve in the middle of a hectic day in which the worst was still ahead.

But Sister Martha recoiled, unsmiling. "To tell you the truth, I haven't been myself for the past couple of days. There's this new girl, Brooke. She's going to be trouble, I can feel it."

"Yes, Brooke Hankey. You know who she is, don't you? Who her father is?"

"No."

"Just don't get in her way, that's all I'm telling you."

"What do you mean?"

Sister Beatrice lifted her eyebrows. Nothing could be said just yet. Best to change the subject. "What's that you're working on?"

Sister Martha held the runner open. "Clemmie asked if I'd fix it."

"Clemmie had Reverend Mother's permission to ask you, of course." Sister Beatrice gave a slow smile.

"You know that crew downstairs. They don't get a whole lot of permission for anything. And they get away with it. I wish I could learn from them."

"Just be careful whom you talk to without permission." Sister Beatrice waved as she left the classroom. She liked Sister Martha, but had to keep in mind that if Reverend Mother were to drag her down—take Sister Martha out of St. Monica's—she herself might be sent away from the school. Or worse still, reassigned as laundress or portress, always under Reverend Mother's nose. A fate worse than death, truly.

When she reached the doorway of her office, she heard the phone ringing.

That afternoon, standing behind the microphone, Sister Beatrice looked out before the assembly of students. All seven hundred of them squirmed and shifted in their uniforms. Chatter and giggles filled the hall, and when she test-touched the crackling microphone, the noise barely stopped. She looked down at Sister Estelle, who was seated at the piano, peering through her eyeglasses at the sheet of music in front of her and talking to Brooke Hankey. Sister Beatrice glared, trying to get the other nun's attention. Sister Estelle kept on talking as if there was nothing more important at the moment than to have a lengthy chat. It was Brooke who finally looked up, and, seeing Sister Beatrice at the microphone, gestured to Sister Estelle, who gave a start and struck the piano keys, producing a crash of chords

The chatter dwindled. Looking down the centre aisle, Sister Beatrice saw the large figure of Reverend Mother appear in the doorway. Earlier this morning, she had fussed over Reverend Mother's chair and its proper location. She remembered from last year's concert that Reverend Mother had seemed dissatisfied with the black leather armchair brought from the principal's office. The superior had spent most of the concert frowning and jamming her elbows into the leather of the arms, as if trying to lower them. This year, through one of the students, Sister Beatrice had borrowed an upholstered chair, the kind that might be found in a parlour, and although the nuns always sat on straight-backed chairs, even when visiting with their families, she thought that Reverend Mother might enjoy the luxury of the upholstered softness. It was royal blue, perhaps a fitting colour. Or perhaps not. There was no way of knowing. She could feel the perspiration dampening the vest under her arms. When would this day be over?

The assembly had fallen quiet, and Sister Beatrice said, "Please rise to welcome our dear and beloved Reverend Mother."

From the side aisles, the nuns gestured to the girls to rise and clap as Reverend Mother walked down the centre aisle and nodded from side to side. Was she perceiving herself as a queen acknowledging her subjects or as the humble Jesus entering Jerusalem to the cries of "Hallelujah"? It was difficult to say: The bowed head suggested she regarded herself with humility, merely carrying out God's will, but the satisfied expression on her face said that the accolade was her due.

Sister Estelle bore down on the piano with fury, the martial music nearly drowned out by the continuous clapping. Sister Beatrice remembered reading in a current affairs pamphlet of an assembly of Soviet generals who refused to stop clapping after a speech by Joseph Stalin because the first one to stop might end up in prison. To banish the thought, she smiled as broadly as she could, holding out her hands in an attempt at a beneficent gesture. Behind Reverend Mother, shuffled Sister Antonetta and the other retired nuns, some with canes, one bent over nearly double. The remnant army of Gideon. Reverend Mother walked directly to the royal blue easy chair and sat down, arranging her habit skirt and rosary beads. She looked pleased with the seat. The other nuns fanned out on either side of her and sat in the straight-backed chairs. From the side aisles, the teaching nuns made gestures for the girls to sit down.

Sister Beatrice's beaming smile remained. When everyone was seated, she faced the figure in the easy chair and said, "Welcome, beloved Reverend Mother, to our feast day concert. This is a bittersweet day, since we've just lost our beloved Holy Father. And yet, we rejoice in honour of Saint Teresa of Avila, your beloved patron."

Reverend Mother nodded, and the nuns seated on either side of her followed suit.

"I now hand the microphone over to Gillian Parker, our student union president," Sister Beatrice continued.

Gillian swept her long hair over her shoulder as she stepped up to the stage and positioned herself behind the microphone. She was short for her years but had an extra serving of aplomb and always did her job well. Sister Beatrice sat down in the front row, her hands shaking. She had planned to use "beloved" only once in her little speech, but no other words came to her as she rattled on. How many unforgiving souls out there, Reverend Mother chief among them, had counted the "beloveds"?

"…And we thank you, Reverend Mother, for this opportunity to perform for you, to share our talents with you on this your special feast day," Gillian concluded. Sister Beatrice was grateful for the girl's confident manner and public speaking ability. She made the school look good.

Gillian returned to her seat and the school choir filed on-stage in two long rows. When they sang Mozart's *Ave Verum Corpus*, Sister Beatrice noticed that Reverend Mother offered a slight smile. A Latin motet, a church piece, was always safe. It was said that Sister Estelle could wrest music from even the most tone deaf in the school. Her choir had taken first prize at the music festival, even though she couldn't be there herself to direct them because of the Holy Rule. That win was a matter of great pride for St. Monica's.

The choir now went on to sing a medley of pretty melodies, and the audience clapped with great enthusiasm. Sister Estelle usually chose well, but it wasn't always clear which songs Reverend Mother would approve of. She had told Sister Beatrice last year that she didn't like "lovey-dovey" songs, but Sister Estelle was so highly regarded that she could get away with having the girls sing romantic pieces such as "Where E'er You Walk." She would simply give the love bits a religious twist—the song was not sung to a human lover but to God. It was always a fine line, though, even for Sister Estelle. Sister Beatrice suspected the other nun feared that Reverend Mother would insist on choosing the songs herself, tuneless things with no harmony.

When it came down to Reverend Mother's preferences, she wanted the concerts to feature girls who might eventually enter the novitiate. "Recruits for Christ," as she liked to describe them. And so here came one of St. Monica's recruits, a girl by the name of Melanie, who played the cello. She was no longer a student, having graduated last year, but she had donned the school uniform for the occasion. She played a deeply beautiful piece that was rich and slow, and then, another song that the girls sitting behind Sister Beatrice seemed to know. She heard someone whisper "Elvis," followed by quiet singing as the cello played: "I want you, I need you, I-hi-hi love you...." For the past couple of years, she had been regularly confiscating pictures of Elvis Presley, that heartthrob with the crooked smile and leering eyes. She glanced over at Reverend Mother, whose big hand was keeping time to the music on her lap, and breathed out slowly, grateful that the song was instrumental and that the cello made it sound like a hymn.

Everyone knew that Melanie would be entering the novitiate in January, so she was held in a kind of awe—her hair, falling to her shoulders, would soon be cut off. She'd be giving up everything that the rest of the girls held dear—clothes, make-up, boyfriends, movies, dances—to give herself to God. Sister Beatrice's body felt rigid, and she flexed her fingers in her lap and pushed her shoulders against the back of her chair in an effort to unwind. She was glad to see Melanie depart the stage.

Next up was a vocal solo. Sister Beatrice shifted in her seat. Sally Sullivan had been set to sing. She had performed recently in a Gilbert and Sullivan revue ("That Sullivan is my great uncle—just kidding," she had said to Sister Beatrice, obviously excited to be chosen). For this concert, she had decided to sing "I'm Called Little Buttercup" from *H.M.S. Pinafore*, one of Sister Estelle's favourites. But then, Brooke Hankey had presented herself at the office this morning, only her second day as a student at St. Monica's, and said, "Sister, may I sing in the concert this afternoon?"

Sister Beatrice had felt her throat tighten. The custom was that only one student in each musical category would perform at the concert so as not to prolong it past Reverend Mother's attention span. "Sally Sullivan is singing at today's concert," she said to Brooke.

Brooke offered no response but remained standing before her.

There was only one thing to do: throw it back to Sister Estelle. "Go over to the convent, ring the front door bell, and ask for Sister Estelle. She'll tell you whether it will be possible for you to sing at the concert." And then, because she couldn't *not* say it: "If she says 'yes' to you, we'll have to say 'no' at the last minute to Sally." She had covered all angles, or so she thought, until Brooke returned, breathless, her dark hair tousled from the wind, and her cheeks high in colour. "Sister Estelle says it's up to you."

Sister Beatrice knew what she had to do. She had to summon Sally to the office. She had to look at her bright, happy face and tell her, with false cheerfulness, "Oh, Sally, there's been a slight change." And she had to watch Sally's smile die.

So now, as a result, here came Brooke up to the stage with her dark eyes and rose-petal cheeks. Sister Estelle played the introductory bars, and the girl began: "*My ship has sails that are made of silk....*'" Her voice was light and not as well-trained as Sally's. She had trouble reaching the occasional high note. "*'But the pearls and such, they won't mean much if there's missing just one thing....*'" Sister Beatrice remembered the song from the radio before she entered the convent. It was pleasant and faintly sad, especially as it ended: "*'If the ship I sing doesn't also bring my own true love to me.*'" The applause was lukewarm. She was a new girl, after all, and most of the students didn't know her. Sally had probably told some of the girls about the last-minute change. The more perceptive among them would soon know the reason.

Sister Beatrice's shoulder twitched and her left hand, which had been in a tight fist, jumped. Her leg was beginning to cramp. She needed to stretch, to move. She turned to Reverend Mother and whispered, "Mother, excuse me, I must check on..." The rest was a deliberate mumble. She stood and slipped down the side aisle.

From the back, the hall's decorations stood out more clearly than they had from the stage. Yesterday, after school, younger nuns with the help of some senior students had set up long tables for today's lunch. They had hung streamers along the walls and across the ceiling: yellow and white, the colours of the papal flag, in honour of the late pope. This would not have been Sister Beatrice's choice, but neither was it a garish colour scheme, and in fact, the tablecloths, white with yellow overlay, had looked downright cheery. She had nearly vetoed the papal flag that they had rigged up at half-mast, and now wished she had. There it stood, sagging in the top left corner of the room. Would Reverend Mother declaim it as a sign of disrespect, limp and insignificant as it was, half-covered by the folds of the stage curtain? She was too weary to worry about the possibility.

Reverend Mother's feast day lunch for the students was always a highlight of the fall term. For the nuns, it meant added work attached to an already stretched schedule, but the students' youthful enthusiasm usually spilled over. The nuns gave a lighthearted impression as they served the lunch, tying back their veils and donning fresh white aprons with bibs. The girls always cheered at the sight of them, transformed as they were from their usual classroom appearance.

Sister Martha, especially, always seemed to be a favourite. There was a great *whoop* as she made her entrance carrying a tray of sandwiches aloft like a servant in ancient Rome, then, after setting them down, holding out her apron skirt like a fan and attempting a clumsy curtsy. She usually spoke to them in pretend Latin combined with old-fashioned English: "Lo, for thy refreshment, delectable *bread-icus cum egg-saladitum et ham-iorum*." The girls would roar, some yelling nonsense back at her: "*Thank-ibus, Sister-oreum*." Once in a while, one would acknowledge her in correct Latin: "*Gratias agimus tibi, Soror!*" and she'd grab her chest in mock surprise and respond with something like, "Send that girl to the top of the class!" Today, however, her smile had been tight and she did not respond when a group of girls called out in happy, jagged voices, "*Sister Martheticum!*" "*Sister Marthalorum!*" When it came to the end of lunch, there was always a rush. The girls were hurried out except for the few designated to help take down the tables and set up the chairs for the afternoon concert. The nuns then had to scramble to choke down a few bites of whatever sandwiches were left. Not a meal to lift anyone's spirits.

Now, in the back row, Sister Martha was surreptitiously cutting thread along the edge of the runner. Most of the cloth remained inside her work-bag, which sat on her lap, its black colour blending into her habit. Sister Beatrice lifted her eyebrows and smiled, hoping the other nun would read her expression as a sign of collusion. But was it merely hypocrisy? Should she avoid Sister Martha altogether?

It was a relief to stand. The cramp in her leg eased. What was so wrong with letting one girl sing instead of another? In the light of eternity, did such a small change merit a second thought? But Sister Martha—that was another question.

Mr. Hankey's voice over the phone had been uncompromising, the voice of a man used to important business dealings in the secular world. "Sister Principal," he had addressed her. Had there been a sneer in his tone? "Macdonald Hankey here."

Macdonald. Ridiculous first name, but likely a familiar one at places where millionaires made their money. She had never spoken to a millionaire before.

Her mouth went dry. "Yes, Mr. Hankey," she croaked. It was important for the school to have girls from well-to-do families. "Good families" was how Reverend Mother referred to them. Girls whose fathers would hand over the money to fix the roof. But millionaires—fathers who would pay for a whole new gymnasium—were rare.

"You're the one I want to talk to. About my daughter, Brooke. As you know, she's new in your school." *Your school.* Not *St. Monica's.* Had he already looked down the list of other possible schools Brooke might go to? "She didn't enroll in your school to be humiliated."

She could hear him breathing. She swallowed. "I don't know what you mean, Mr. Hankey." She sounded like a small child about to be slapped.

"I expect that the teachers are going to teach what they're supposed to, and that they are going to keep classes under control. That Latin teacher..." His voice had a hard edge.

"Latin? Oh, you must mean Sister Martha." She was immediately sorry for mentioning the other nun's name. Best for all to remain nameless. She had no idea what he was talking about.

"Yesterday was Brooke's first day at your school, and that nun singled her out. Humiliated her and said some shocking things that I won't repeat. Obscene things."

"Obscene? Mr. Hankey, I'm sure there must be an explanation…"

"That nun should be sacked."

"I'll speak to—to that teacher. Yes, I'll do that. I'm so sorry." Her hand had shaken as she replaced the receiver.

She blinked as she brought herself back to Reverend Mother's feast-day concert. Thankfully, it concluded with no mishap. At the front of the room, Reverend Mother was climbing the stairs leading to the stage with Gillian's help. She herself should have been up there to accompany the superior. Sister Beatrice made a mental note—she must single out that girl for special praise. She had helped save the day twice now.

She walked back up the aisle on tiptoes and resumed her seat. She knew that she must speak to Reverend Mother. What choice did she have?

"There are many ways to be a saint," Reverend Mother said into the microphone. "How many of you are familiar with the life of my patron, the great Saint Teresa of Avila?" Hands went up across the assembly. She began more or less this way every year. "Saint Teresa was originally a girl just like you, just like I was, as all the nuns were at one time." She spread her large bony hands, as if to embrace everyone in the room. "And did she want to join the convent? I should say she did not. But did she answer God's call? Yes, she did. She had headaches and all sorts of heavy burdens—nuns who wouldn't obey her orders, and so she had to punish them. And through it all she became a saint. She was a great spiritual guide. She went into ecstasies when she prayed. Sometimes, she even levitated. Now, I don't expect that any of us are going to levitate one of these days, but you never know."

There was a general murmur, but Sister Beatrice didn't know if the girls were amused at Reverend Mother's attempt at humour or if they were merely restless. Reverend Mother pressed her fingertips together and continued: "Some of you too will be called to be nuns." She pulled from her pocket a leather-covered book. "This is my patron's autobiography," she said, opening it to a marked place, and reading: "'What terrible harm is wrought in religious when the religious life is not properly observed; when of the two paths that can be followed in a religious house—one leading to virtue and the observance of the Rule and the other leading away from the Rule—both are frequented almost equally!'" Reverend Mother ran her finger along the page, looking confused, as if she had lost her place. The shifting throughout the assembly had increased, and whispering had begun here and there. Sister Beatrice sprang to her feet and climbed up to the stage. She was aware of her burning cheeks as she leaned into the microphone to speak. "Thank you so very much, Reverend Mother." How noticeable was her false enthusiasm?

When Reverend Mother and the old nuns had returned to the convent and the last of the students had left the school, Sister Beatrice walked down the corridor to Sister Martha's room. It was only fair to tell her that Mr. Hankey had called and that she had no choice but to report this matter to Reverend Mother.

Sister Martha's room was empty. The opportunity was lost. She turned back, her soft footsteps the only sound. The school's stillness made her shiver, and she quickened her pace to the door leading back to the convent.

7. The Oil of Gladness

SISTER MARTHA HURRIED WITH HUNCHED shoulders along the path between the school and the convent, holding her briefcase with a white-knuckled hand, her face tight and hemmed in by the stiffness of the wimple. The weather had taken a turn during the day, the wind whipping leaves off the trees. The bushes in the rose garden had lost most of their blooms, leaving bare stems and thorns. Approaching the back door of the convent, she straightened her shoulders, shifted her briefcase to her other hand, and forced her lips into a smile.

The smile was short-lived. There had been none of the usual camaraderie with the girls for the past few days. She had felt testy throughout the day, ignoring the girl who passed her on the stairs and said, "How's it going today, Sister?" The greeting agitated her. Did the girl see that she wasn't herself? She would normally say, "Couldn't be better, thanks be to God," and finger a bead of the large rosary that hung from her waist. Then she might tease, "Are you trying to butter me up for tomorrow's quiz?" The girls knew perfectly well what was expected of them, but they were also aware that Sister Martha liked them.

What they didn't know was that Reverend Mother's feast day was more of a penance than a pleasure for the nuns. If the superior didn't like the program or the manners of the students, who knew where the axe would fall? Reverend Mother had once humiliated an excellent choir teacher in front of the whole school because of the words "true love" in the harmless Christmas song, "Tomorrow Shall Be My Dancing Day."

It had been a trying couple of days—the unnerving new girl, Brooke, and Gina with her smirking comments about how the Holy Father's body was embalmed—it was one thing after another. And then this afternoon seeing Brooke on the stage singing the solo in a cracked soprano instead of Sally Sullivan, whom everyone knew to be the finest singer in the school—who was this girl, that she held such sway? And what was it that Sister Beatrice had said about the girl's father? Making her way downstairs to the basement common room, Sister Martha felt alone, with nothing to hold onto.

She took her place at her desk in the common room, setting her tattered briefcase beside her on the floor. She placed her black sewing work-bag onto her lap. Outside the window, rain was beginning to fall. The sound of shuffling bodies surrounded her, and from one corner, an occasional bronchial cough. Desks formed a ring around the common room, one behind another, like horses on a merry-go-round. A few days earlier, she had turned hers to face the wall to avoid the smells emanating from the posterior of the nun in front of her. She hadn't asked permission to make this move; she simply went ahead and felt a pleasing burst of independence when she actually got away with it. Reverend Mother seemed not to notice. She might notice other, smaller things that were off-kilter, such as a crooked bandeau or a prayer book on the pew ledge with the pages, rather than the book's spine, facing outward. Were her eyes getting too weak to see anything not directly in front of her? Or was her mind now fixed mostly on minutiae? Sister Clementia was the only one who seemed aware of the desk change, and when the little lay sister had come by with her mop and duster, Sister Martha whispered, "Leave my desk like this, Clemmie." Sister Clementia was a good sort, keeping things to herself. She expressed neither surprise nor annoyance at the new desk position. "Very well, Sister," she muttered, not even looking up.

Sister Martha put her work-bag inside the desk and flicked through her first-year Latin textbook, pausing at the pages with pictures. It was a stalling tactic, a means of putting off planning tomorrow's classes. She had no interest in Roman drinking cups or sketches of Gallic warriors. The pictures of mosaics, however, drew her in every time she flipped through the textbook. She stopped now, as she usually did, at the mosaic of a dog. "*Cave Canem*," the inscription read. "Beware the dog." A chain leash attached to the dog's collar held its head back. Its body was taut, its claws long and sharp, its teeth bared. The dog's ears stood on end; the eye in its profiled face was savage and angry. It stared at her from the page, that eye, making her flinch. She lifted her thumb, and several pages flew by. She stopped at the place marked by her mother's mortuary card, the page where yesterday's lesson had ended. The mosaic of the cockfight always unnerved her most of all. The beasts faced each other with feathers raised and spindly legs on the point of leaping, their fierce eyes and shaking combs the signal that they were set to rip one another apart. "A lively cockfight drew an audience in Rome...."

She lifted the mortuary card. She could still see her mother, plump and friendly, dark hair pulled back, a gold filling flashing at the corner of her mouth when she laughed. It was an insult to have left her mortuary card on the same page as the fighting cocks. She slipped it inside the back cover.

She scanned the chapter's vocabulary, then glanced at the next section, "Latin in English." "'*Via*' has a number of interesting derivatives. 'Trivial' is made up of the prefix 'tri-', meaning 'three', and 'via'. It referred originally to the point where three roads meet. At such crossroads the nearby people would meet and gossip about the happenings of the neighbourhood. Thus 'trivial' came to mean 'unimportant.'"

She lifted the lid of her desk to fetch a pencil. Just inside, sat a movie magazine she had confiscated from one of the students several days earlier. *Silver Screen*. The girls were forever reading these things, the nuns forever confiscating them. A favourite trick of the students, and one of the easiest to spot, was to prop up a textbook at the head of the desk during study hall time and to turn the pages of the magazine while pretending to be studying. When Sister Martha came down the aisle, the girl would be too engrossed in the magazine to notice until it was too late.

The offense took place so frequently that she simply held her hand out, giving the culprit a deadpan look. In days gone by, such girls had stood a good chance of being expelled or at least receiving a stern warning. Nowadays, however, like lipstick and transistor radios, the crime drew nothing more serious than a look of mock exasperation. The girl had only to relinquish the offending object, or wipe off her lipstick with a tissue, and the world was set aright again.

Sister Martha slipped the magazine out of the desk, pulled some test papers out of her briefcase and placed them over the cover. She looked around. No one was looking at her, of course. Why would they? She stood up, picked up her desk, and set it back down in proper formation. Much better, the way of conformity; there'd be no chance of someone walking by and looking over her shoulder. The leg of the desk banged against her chair, and she silently cursed her clumsiness. She walked over to a bookshelf and hesitated in front of the largest book. Was it right to use the Bible for camouflage? She pulled it down, scanning the rest of the room. No one looked up. She sat down, opened the Bible somewhere in the middle, and slipped the magazine inside.

As a teenager, she had known all the movie stars. When the family went into town, she spent as much time as she could get away with reading the movie magazines in the drugstore. Now, as she turned the pages, the faces were from a different world. Women with tight pants that went down just below the knee, their waists tiny. Slender as reeds. Handsome young men in bathing trunks against an ocean backdrop. She recognized Cary Grant on one page. He looked older than she remembered him. But of course. She hadn't remained a teenager herself, had she? When she came upon a series of photographs of Elizabeth Taylor with her baby, she didn't need a caption to tell her who the beautiful woman was—the same dark eyebrows, the lovely smile, the perfect features. She wore a flowing dressing gown, and the infant was tenderly nestled in her arms. But the eyes—they were not the eyes of the girl in *National Velvet*. Well, hadn't Elizabeth Taylor matured just like everyone else? She wasn't going to remain an innocent young girl forever. But no—there was a guardedness in the eyes that turned the picture of maternal beauty into something else. Something wary, even hard.

Sister Martha looked up at the wall ahead. A framed, cross-stitched hanging contained the words of St. Teresa: "Let nothing disturb thee, let nothing affright thee. God alone suffices." The picture was always crooked. Sister Antonetta, who had nothing better to do except report to Reverend Mother on everyone else's infractions, was forever heaving herself up on a chair, trying in vain to put it right.

Sister Martha didn't really mind the sentiment expressed in the cross-stitch. It wasn't Saint Teresa's fault that she carried the burden of being Reverend Mother's patron saint. Crooked or not, here was the bare-bones truth of their lives: Their sole purpose was to please God alone. Pondering this truth always brought her up short. But was the infinite mind of God really filtered through the crooked mind of Reverend Mother, as they'd been taught?

She heard the sound of a rosary and the soft tread of rubber-soled shoes close to her, and she looked up to see the black figure of Sister Julianne. The other nun beckoned to her. Sister Martha closed the Bible over the magazine and stood up, hesitating. She couldn't leave the Bible on her desk like that, with the flashy edges of the movie magazine sticking out. She did an awkward half-turn, hiding the desk with the bulk of her habit, slipped the magazine back inside, and returned the Bible to the shelf. She followed the other nun to the door. "Reverend Mother would like to see you, Sister," Sister Julianne said once they were in the corridor. She put her finger to her lips and walked away. Sister Martha did a rapid scan of the day now nearing its end. A few mishaps and misdemeanours could have caught Reverend Mother's attention. Which one was it now?

Walking up the back staircase to the first floor and stopping briefly at the chapel to genuflect and dip her fingers in the holy water font before obeying the summons felt like the ritual march to the executioner. Except that with the executioner, the march would never again be repeated. The summons to Reverend Mother's office would go on again and again for the rest of Sister Martha's life, or at least until she reached a state of such senility that a summons didn't matter anymore. The sign of the cross at times like this, the dampness lingering lightly on her forehead, was the most fervent of the day. *What have I done wrong?* Walking along the polished corridor, the padding of her own footsteps the only sound, she tried to affect an exasperated nonchalance: *All right. What now?* The pretence didn't work.

Sister Beatrice stood in the doorway of Reverend Mother's office. She turned to Sister Martha, reddening slightly and averting her eyes. This involuntary blushing, Sister Martha noticed, always happened whenever the principal seemed to feel she had been caught. She slipped past Sister Martha into the corridor, leaving the door open. Sister Martha knocked on the open door.

"Come in, Sister," Reverend Mother said. She sat upright looking at the papers on her desk, her face set in its usual leathery pattern. "Sit down."

Sister Martha bowed and sat down in the straight-backed chair opposite the desk. This was one of those times when she regretted her own girth. She wanted, when confronting Reverend Mother, to be small and slight, a waif on the edge of the chair, her demeanour begging for pity. Instead, she was too heavy to sit exactly on the edge, and she felt ridiculous in her flabbiness. "Sister Marshmallow," she'd heard one of the girls say, referring to her.

"Sister Beatrice received a complaint today from the father of one of the girls," Reverend Mother said. She looked up from the papers on her desk only when she had finished speaking.

Sister Martha's heart raced as her mind flitted through the day. She looked steadily at Reverend Mother, saying nothing. She felt proud of her self-control. Often, in her nervousness, she blabbered when she should have kept her mouth shut.

"Yesterday was the girl's first day at school. Her name is Brooke Hankey. You know who her father is?"

Sister Martha's throat felt dry. "No, Mother." The words were cracked and low.

"Well, I suppose I wouldn't expect you to know." Always this poke in the ribs, a reference to a more-than-modest farm upbringing. A peasant. With a non-Catholic father. "Mr. Hankey is our most important benefactor. He owns—well, you needn't know all that. Sister Beatrice was happy to take in the girl this late in the school term because he said he'd provide funding for the gymnasium. Now, it seems, after the first day, he's decided that St. Monica's may not be the school he wants for his daughter." She looked hard at Sister Martha now, a cold stare. "Because of the antics of the girl's Latin teacher."

"I don't know what you mean, Mother." Sister Martha blinked and stared at Reverend Mother. The superior's eyes were impenetrable.

"Some disgusting comments were made?" Reverend Mother's large brown hands rested on a small pile of papers in front of her. "Comments unbecoming of a nun. And you called the girl names, embarrassing her. Making fun of her." The superior's thin, white lips barely moved.

A knot tightened in Sister Martha's stomach. "I, I don't know what you're talking about, Mother."

"You don't remember that the class was out of control? That the girls were laughing among themselves, and *you* were laughing with them? You don't remember that you scolded this girl Brooke in front of the whole class and that you called her uncharitable names?"

Sister Martha's ears pounded. The superior had the power to take her away from the girls of St. Monica's. These were the only people who mattered to her, even if some of them called her, "Sister Marshmallow." Reverend Mother had the power to put her into a kindergarten class of screaming brats, or into the laundry, or into the library where she would twiddle her thumbs all day and rub shoulders with the likes of Sister Antonetta and slowly grow stupid and senile. Who'd have thought she'd be brought to this point by the angel-faced Brooke?

Perspiration trickled down the side of her face. She longed to wipe it with her finger but dared not. She kept her hands folded on her lap. Reverend Mother had this power because the Church said so. She was the voice of God, the living image of God's will. So said the Holy Rule: "The Sisters shall open their hearts with all simplicity to their Superior as the representative of Christ." She would open her heart and explain the misunderstanding in the class and the later outburst to Gina. "It was the chapter on the vocative case, Mother." She tried to smile, but the muscles in her face twitched. "There were pictures that some of the girls found funny." What more could she say?

"They said disgusting things, and you did nothing to rebuke them."

"Actually I did, Mother. I tried to get their attention back...."

Reverend Mother looked hard at her. Sister Martha knew immediately it had been wrong to contradict her. "Today's gospel reading—have you forgotten it so soon? The wise and foolish virgins?"

"Mother." She hated to say it, but it was true. "I didn't understand what they were laughing at, and I didn't know what
to do about it. And about the things I said to those two girls,
I'm very sorry...."

"It's obvious which of the two you are, the wise or the foolish."

Sister Martha's mind went back to the summer's retreat,
when a red-faced priest had told the community of nuns in a
booming voice that they were to consider the leaves and aphids
on a tree. Which did they resemble? A healthy leaf or an aphid?

"You know what an aphid does. An aphid sucks the life
out of a plant. An aphid is good-for-nothing. Now, let us ask
ourselves: I, who have given my life to the service of God—am
I becoming more Christ-like, have I spent myself sufficiently
in His service, or have I become like a fat aphid, destroying
the life around me?"

She had tried to avoid thinking about the question, but "I
am a fat aphid" had swirled around her mind like a mantra
for days afterward. Now it was the wise and foolish virgins
from today's gospel. "Give us of your oil, for our lamps have
gone out," the foolish virgins had said. Reverend Mother was
right. Her lamp had gone out.

Reverend Mother's voice droned on: "Mr. Hankey may take
the girl out of St. Monica's if he can find another school that
will take her this late in the term. If that happens...."

Where had she begun to go wrong? Using a Bible to hold
a magazine showing frivolous lives. That action revealed
everything about her. She was a fraud encased in a religious
habit, pretending to live a holy life. Grasping onto the love
of her girls in St. Monica's as if their acceptance was all that
mattered. When had morning meditation become a time when
she planned her classes for the day ahead? When had prayer
become meaningless? She remembered the missal's commen-
tary on today's feast: "For long years, St. Teresa endured
dryness in prayer and infirmity in body, and God rewarded
her...." She couldn't remember the rest. If she learned to pray

again, perhaps there was a chance for her. If she learned to see God in the leathery face before her.

"Mother, can I make reparation for this in some way?" Sister Martha asked, her hands tightly clasped.

"Mr. Hankey is going to buy us a statue of Saint Teresa. Made in Spain. We'll put it in front of the convent." She pulled a glossy catalogue from the pile of papers, turned to a page that had been marked, and gazed at it.

Sister Martha sat forward. "But, Mother, isn't he paying for the new gymnasium?"

Reverend Mother's face hardened again, her lips a horizontal line. "Who told you that?" Her voice was sharp.

Sister Martha's head began to pound against her bandeau. "You said..."

"A gymnasium," the superior whispered to herself, looking at the catalogue. "We're in a rudderless ship. The barque of St. Peter has no captain. The whole Church is adrift. Religious life has gone soft. Silence no longer kept among the nuns. Disobedience everywhere. Whom can I count on to be obedient? No one." Her voice was flat.

Sister Martha felt her stomach tighten. "Mother, I don't think that's..."

Reverend Mother looked straight at her. "In times past, they took years to elect a new Holy Father. *Years.* There were factions among the cardinals and even *wars.* I fear it is like that now." She held out her big hands, palms up, the fingers spread open. "They will leave us adrift for years."

"Oh, Mother, that was long ago. There are no factions now. The Holy Spirit is among the cardinals, and they're all unified. We'll have a new Holy Father soon."

Reverend Mother looked at her with hooded eyes that seemed to pore right through her. She knew exactly what Sister Martha was made of. Marshmallow.

"Give me an account of yourself," the superior was saying. "Your days and weeks and years."

"An account, Mother?" Sister Martha said. "I don't know what you mean."

Reverend Mother's wrinkles contracted into a sour expression. "'I don't know what you mean,'" she said in a squeaky voice. She continued in her normal tone: "I meant what I said. Am I speaking a language you don't understand?"

"I've always done my best, Mother." Her throat was constricted, and her legs felt as if they might crumble.

"'I've always done my best, Mother.'" Again, the sour look and the mocking voice.

Sister Martha felt tears forming behind her eyes. It was best to keep control of herself. Remain silent, a sacrificial lamb.

"You've been nothing but a bad influence on the students. Instead of being an influence for good, you've led them astray. And as for our religious community, you're good-for-nothing. A lukewarm example. You know what God says about lukewarm souls. 'I will vomit them out of my mouth.' Have you meditated on this? What have you to say for yourself?"

Sister Martha adjusted her posture and kept her eyes on the superior's face.

"You don't like hearing this, do you?" Reverend Mother stared back at her. "You want to hear that you're an excellent example to others. You don't like to hear that you're vomit, that you should be cast out of this community and out of St. Monica's School."

Sister Martha shifted her gaze away from Reverend Mother to the window. The rain had stopped, and beyond the iron gates, two St. Monica's girls were flanked by a trio of St. Paul's boys. They crossed the street and disappeared, as free and unconcerned as you please. She smiled at Reverend Mother and said, "Thank you, Mother. May I go now?"

The superior appeared to soften. "Go on your way. You're a poor excuse for a nun."

She waved her hand and Sister Martha left the office. On her way to the common room, she went into the chapel and took the daily missal from her place. Downstairs, seated at her desk, she opened it to October 15, the feast of St. Teresa, and read: "In accomplishing the reform, St. Teresa lacked all human support and had to endure many contradictions." Then, she turned to the prayers and readings from today's Mass. "*Dilexisti justitiam, et odisti iniquitatem.*" "You have loved justice and hated evil. Therefore, God has anointed you with the oil of gladness."

Back in the common room, she opened her desk, pushed aside the movie magazine and books, and took out her work-bag. As she opened it, she could hear Reverend Mother's voice. "I will vomit them out of my mouth."

8. Morning Drink

SISTER ANTONETTA STOPPED AT THE kitchen doorway, listening, with the bishop's breakfast tray in her hands. The bishop had said Mass for the nuns this morning, and after his breakfast, he'd left the parlour to make his thanksgiving in chapel before his meeting with Reverend Mother. She'd had the privilege of picking up his tray.

There were murmurings inside the kitchen, but nothing she could hear distinctly. They might be saying the rosary. That's what Sister Kate would say—"We're on the second sorrowful mystery, the scourging at the pillar, Sister. Is there something you wanted?" Sister Kate always had a way of getting out of any trap she might be in—breaking silence, to be exact. It was Sister Antonetta's role to make sure that the whole community kept silence as it should be kept, with nothing said without permission. That was another thing about Sister Kate—she often said she had permission to speak when Sister Antonetta was quite sure that no permission had been granted.

From the doorway, she couldn't tell what was going on, and so she stepped inside. Sister Kate, her veil flecked with flour and her bandeau crooked, stood at the big black stove, stirring the contents of a pot. The short one, Sister Clementia, was outside shaking the dust mop. If they'd been praying the rosary, it had, for some reason, stopped.

She set the tray on the sideboard and turned to Sister Kate. She'd been waiting for this moment ever since she noticed the

nuns' marmalade in the crystal dish on the bishop's tray. It was
the lumpy marmalade, the kind with oranges that had been
all whirled up together into a pulp and thrown into large cans
like the one that sat on the sideboard just now. The priest's
marmalade, called "Golden Peel," had lovely thin slices of peel
floating in clear jelly. But the Golden Peel jar was missing from
the shelf above the sideboard. Where was it? Had they used
it to feed that woman Lizzie in the pantry? No, surely. Had
she herself taken it somewhere? Had she put it in the library?

It was a point of pride for her that she had the charge of
picking up the priest's breakfast tray from the parlour every
morning after he departed. She, of course, never encountered
the priest himself. But she washed and dried his dishes—her
family's fragile china with the delicate pink roses, the silver
toast tray, and little coffee pot—and she had permission to
take the tray cloth to the laundry if it became soiled. She knew
exactly where that jar of Golden Peel marmalade should be.

"She'll be Mrs. Mucky-muck today with the bishop's tray."
It was little Sister Clementia coming back inside, holding the
dust mop. She stopped abruptly when she saw Sister Antonetta.
She pushed up her thick spectacles and made her way to the
broom closet. Silence filled the kitchen, punctuated only by
the scraping of Sister Kate's large spoon against the bottom
of the pot.

Sister Antonetta didn't have permission to speak, but there
was nothing for it but to point out the error. She held up the
crystal dish with its lumpy contents. "This is the nuns' marmalade. The ordinary one. This is not what should be given to
the bishop." She wasn't sure which of the two nuns she should
be addressing, and so she looked from one to the other. "Why
wasn't the bishop given the priest's marmalade?" She held
herself up straight, glad to be able to teach these two a lesson.

Sister Clementia peered at the dish as if she had never laid
eyes on such a thing before. "We're out of the other," she said
finally.

Sister Kate laughed. "You're holding that thing up like the priest at the consecration."

"It's no laughing matter that we gave the bishop less than the best. Reverend Mother won't be happy to find out…"

"Sister, there was none of the priest's marmalade left," Sister Clementia said.

"And whose fault is that?" Sister Antonetta opened the large marmalade can and scraped the pulpy contents of the crystal dish into it.

From outside came the sound of a truck along the gravel, followed soon by the delivery man's voice. Sister Kate turned from the stove and wiped her hands on her blue apron. Sister Clementia, rushing to the door, called, "Is it yourself, Peter?" Just like that, as if the man were a personal friend.

From the sink, where she was washing the bishop's dishes, Sister Antonetta turned and watched as the man carried boxes inside. He had a ruddy face and hair plastered down on his head and wore blue overalls. Sister Clementia read aloud the label on each box, and Sister Kate checked the items off a list. "One box of tinned jam." "One ten-pound box of tea…."

"Kate, do you see the Golden Peel marmalade at all?" she heard Sister Clementia say. "Kate." Not even giving the cook the respect of her title, "Sister." The thin edge of the wedge. That's what Reverend Mother liked to say. Give them an inch and they'll take a mile. "That's why we keep religious decorum under control," she liked to say. "There must be obedience and modesty, so that this convent is always a model of perfect order." If Reverend Mother knew the half of what went on in this kitchen. "Peter." "Kate." As if they were just people in the world going about their own business.

She heard Sister Kate laugh. "What did I tell you, Clemmie? She forgot to order it."

Laughing at her, Sister Antonetta. Was she not a spouse of Christ just as they were? But had she really forgotten to order the priest's marmalade? Or had she ordered it and put it somewhere for safekeeping, so that they couldn't get their hands on it?

She finished washing and drying the dishes from the bishop's tray, put them carefully in the brown cupboard, and went upstairs. It was time for her visit to chapel.

It was always pleasant during her morning visit to see the novices running the mop up and down the chapel aisles, bending and dusting the pews, disappearing and reappearing, their white veils tied behind their shoulders, their youthful bodies up and down like jack-in-the-boxes. She herself sat stiffly, hard against the back of the pew. She must have been like them once, so ready to do God's will, so keen on obedience. She saw the face of a novice just now, a few pews ahead. The dark eyebrows and rosy plump cheeks made her think of a picture of St. Thérèse, the Little Flower, all bundled up in her new habit, hanging on to the big cross, a shy smile on her face.

All very well for her, saint and all that she was. Entered the convent at fifteen and died at twenty-four. Who wouldn't still be holy at twenty-four? Let the youngster live another forty or fifty years, and see then how saintly she is. Would she still consider drops of water from her neighbour in the laundry to be little jewels of grace sent from God? More than likely, no. She'd be more inclined to splash some water back, teach the neighbour a lesson.

The green cloth covering the altar was crooked. Why on earth couldn't it be made straight? If she tried to get the attention of the novice bobbing up and down in front of her, would that be an infraction against the Holy Rule? At any rate, the youngster was so blessedly modest, she wouldn't have looked up if a bat had swooped down upon her. There was nothing to be done but to try and ignore the crooked altar covering and concentrate on the russet chrysanthemum plant in front of Our Lady's statue. Russet, the least attractive colour for chrysanthemums.

When she finished her five decades of the rosary, she went up the side aisle to the top of the chapel to begin her daily stations of the cross. The stations were a drudgery for her, and yet they had to be done. Worse still, when the novices were in the chapel, she had to look recollected and pious, as if she were in deep meditative reverie over the passion and death of Our Lord Jesus Christ. Moving from station to station, genuflecting. "We adore Thee O Christ and we praise Thee, because by Thy holy Cross Thou hast redeemed the world." She had long since become wearied of those words. As seemly as she could, she moved from one station to another: Jesus falls the first time; Jesus meets His mother; Veronica wipes His holy Face Then genuflecting in the centre aisle and moving to the other side of the chapel. Jesus meets the women of Jerusalem, who wear sombre-coloured cloaks and weep at the sight of Him because of the crown of thorns on his head and drops of blood on his face. Sister Antonetta was always irritated by the red paint dabbed onto Jesus's face, as if the artist had just let the paintbrush drip. She had said once at recreation, "Why can't the artist make a reasonable facsimile of drops of blood?" and Reverend Mother had fixed her with her eye, sending a chill down her back. It was one of the rare occasions when she misspoke.

At the tenth station, where Jesus is stripped of His garments, she wondered if she might get a chance to see the bishop in the sacristy. She craned her neck to the sacristy door. But of course, he would, by now, be meeting with Reverend Mother in the parlour. She wished she'd been asked to bring him his breakfast tray. She didn't know why this privilege was never given to her. Oh, it was fine for her to iron Reverend Mother's newspaper, to bring Reverend Mother's tray with its bacon and toast to the refectory each morning. Why couldn't she bring the priest's tray to him in the parlour? Could she not smile and say, "Good morning, Father" to the priest? Could she not be counted on to hold the tray steady, with modesty and grace, without spilling the coffee or the cream? If she had been allowed to take up the bishop's tray this morning, she would have noticed that the marmalade was the inferior sort, and she would have made sure that it had been replaced. But where was the Golden Peel now? A novice passed close to her, cleaning the radiator with a feather duster. Sister Antonetta stood up straight and moved her lips as if in silent prayer.

Kneeling at the communion rail after she had finished the stations, she drew out her pocket watch. It was nearly ten o'clock, almost time for Reverend Mother's morning drink. She genuflected and left the chapel.

Approaching the kitchen, she heard voices coming from the pantry across the hall. The woman Lizzie. Having her morning tea and cigarette, chattering like a fishwife.

"Nobody told me he was in the parlour, the bishop!" Lizzie was saying. "And he was that quiet, there was no sound at all."

Peeking inside the pantry door, Sister Antonetta saw Sister Kate wipe her hands with a towel. "What did you do, Lizzie?" the cook asked.

"I begun to dust the side tables, and just as I'm doing that, the door at the other end opens and there comes in Reverend Mother! And I look up, and he's sitting there in the brown leather chair with his purple hat on."

"Purple hat?" It was a man's voice. The delivery man. Peter, as they called him. They must have given him a cup of tea. The downstairs of the convent had become a restaurant where men and all sorts could come in for tea. It was no longer a religious house down here. She held back.

"The little beanie they wear on top of their head," Lizzie was saying. "And I see Reverend Mother kneel down and he holds up his hand and she kisses his ring. It was a great enormous purple ring, it was." Sister Antonetta peered around the corner of the doorway and saw Lizzie twisting the fingers of one hand around the ring finger of the other. "I've never seen anything like it! The Reverend Mother kissing the bishop's ring!"

Sister Antonetta saw Sister Kate sit down across from Lizzie. "Did you hear what they were talking about?" she said.

"He says, 'Reverend Mother,' and then he coughs," Lizzie continued. "And then he says, 'Your community.' Then he coughs again. And Reverend Mother is bent over, as if she's listening to every gargle of his throat. I'm sorry, Sister, I shouldn't say that. They're two great people talking to each other. He says, 'Your rule,' like that. 'Your *rule*.' And things I didn't understand. 'Sisters must breathe,' says he."

"'Sisters must breathe'?" Sister Kate said.

"Yes, and Holy Ghost and your Holy Rule. I must say it sounded nonsense—oh, I don't mean that, Sister, it surely wasn't nonsense. 'The spirit of the Holy Rule' he says."

"What did Reverend Mother say?"

"I couldn't hear, her voice was that low. Oh, Sister, I shouldn't be speaking out of turn like this. Especially…"

Sister Antonetta shifted her feet outside the door, and all became silent. There was nothing for it but to enter the pantry. Sister Kate stood and took down a large can of vegetables from a shelf and said, "Yes, Sister?"

"I've come to get Reverend Mother's morning drink. She would like apple juice."

She followed the cook into the kitchen, feeling sorry to have been heard outside the pantry. She would have liked to hear what else Lizzie had to say about Reverend Mother and the bishop. What would she herself have done if she'd been in Lizzie's place? Would she have continued on, made herself small amid the legs of the furniture, pretending to be dusting, but listening to their conversation, or would she stand, modestly and humbly of course, and say, "Good morning, Your Excellency, excuse me"?

Sister Kate set the can on the table and went for Reverend Mother's tray.

Just then, the delivery man came through the kitchen on his way out. "Cheerio, Sisters, I'll be off now. That's the lot.

Thanks for the tea." He put on his cap and left.

"Right you are, Peter," Sister Kate called after him on her way to the walk-in refrigerator.

Sister Antonetta glanced back. The cook had momentarily disappeared inside the cooler. With no one looking, she tiptoed out the back door. The man had opened the back gate and was getting into his truck. "Sir!" she called to him.

The man stopped and climbed down from the truck. "Hello, Sister." He pulled off his cap, leaving a string of hair hanging over one ear.

She took a step closer to him. She didn't want to venture too far away from the door. Windows, after all, lined the sides of the convent, and who knew who was looking out just at that moment? Custody of the eyes required that the nuns never ventured to a window simply to look idly out at the world, but one never knew. "Sir, I want to ask about the order today. About the marmalade."

"The marmalade, Sister?" The man had a pleasant face.

"Yes. I don't know if I ordered the Golden Peel. Perhaps I did, and you forgot to deliver it?"

The man reached into the cab of the truck and pulled out a clipboard. "Let me see." He ran his finger down the board. He had a workman's hand that Sister Antonetta wouldn't have minded stroking, just to get the feel of it. It would have some roughness, for sure, but perhaps inside the palm would be soft.

"There's no marmalade by that name. Golden Peel, you say?"

"Yes, we get small jars of it." She held one hand above the other, in such a way as to indicate the size of the jar. The smallness of it, in contrast to the large cans that he delivered routinely, would indicate the importance of the commodity. "It's the best marmalade. It's a golden colour, and there are the smallest shreds of pure Seville oranges floating in the jelly. It's for the priest, who has breakfast here after Mass, and today we had the bishop, only we didn't have any Golden Peel this morning."

"I don't see it here. You're sure you ordered it?" The delivery man frowned, a solicitous look on his face. He put the clipboard back on the seat of the truck and rolled up one of his sleeves, showing a plump arm covered in nice dark hairs.

"I know I ordered it!" She took a step toward him.

He seemed to shrink away as he climbed into the truck. "I'd best be on my way, Sister. Don't know anything about that marmalade. If you order it, I'll get it for you next week."

"Where will you be that I can order it?"

He started up the truck and rolled down the window. She began to walk beside the slowly moving vehicle.

"Do the usual. Let Kate know." He waved his hand out the window and sped up. The gravel in the driveway spat up bits of stones

Kate.

When she returned to the kitchen, Reverend Mother's drink of apple juice was sitting in a tray along with some biscuits on a china plate. In the meantime, Sister Virginia, all white-draped in her infirmarian's habit, was setting up another tray in silence.

Sister Kate was opening the can of vegetables. She pointed to the apple juice. "There's Reverend Mother's drink. But Sister Virginia just said she'll be having morning tea with the bishop."

Sister Antonetta bristled. "She will not. If you remember, we don't eat with secular people."

Sister Kate carried the opened can to the stove. "The bishop isn't secular people."

Sister Clementia was peeling vegetables at the far end of the kitchen. "Reverend Mother can eat with whoever she likes," she muttered.

Sister Antonetta turned sharply to her. "I heard that. Reverend Mother keeps the Holy Rule along with everyone else. Except for some people I know."

Sister Virginia had placed two china cups and saucers and a plate of toast fingers and cakes on the tray. She continued to move about in silence.

"If she wasn't going to have her morning drink as usual, she would have told me," Sister Antonetta said. "It's my duty to take it up to her, unless she tells me otherwise." She picked up the tray with the apple juice and biscuits and left the kitchen.

Upstairs, the parlour door was closed. She held her ear to the door. Reverend Mother spoke with a mannish voice, and so it was impossible to tell who was speaking. The sounds of the kitchen were still in her ears. "Reverend Mother can eat with whoever she likes."

"Excuse me, Sister," a voice said right behind her. Sister Antonetta jumped. Sister Virginia, always sour-faced, stood holding the other tray. A silver teapot had joined the two china cups and saucers and the plate of toast fingers and cakes.

"Who's that for?" Sister Antonetta asked.

Sister Virginia kept her eyes cast down and gestured her out of the way. She knocked at the door and entered the parlour. Sister Antonetta looked down at the tray in her hands. Juice bubbles were still dissolving at the edge of the glass.

She continued along the corridor to Reverend Mother's office. She stopped outside the office door, looked up and down the corridor, knocked gently, and pretended to listen for the voice within. Then she opened the door. The room's silence almost overtook her. She had never before been in Reverend Mother's office when it was empty. She looked at the big wooden desk with its black crucifix and the day's newspaper and mail. Then she turned her eyes to the chair with its leather seat and smooth brown arms.

"Your drink, Mother," she said to the empty chair. She put the tray down on the desk and sat on the chair, rubbing her hands along its smooth arms. The newspaper, which she had ironed this morning, bore the headline, "Pope's Doctor Departs for U.S.," and underneath was a picture of the doctor, bespectacled and moustachioed, looking like a gangster. She pushed the newspaper aside. The morning's mail was stacked neatly on the corner of the desk. The mail came in a bag that was delivered to the front door, and she brought the bag to Reverend Mother's office every morning. That was the last she ever saw of any mail until, of course, the rare times when a thin letter appeared on her desk in the common room. Her parents were long dead and only a distant cousin bothered to write. She would dearly have loved to be taken into Reverend Mother's confidence sufficiently to help her with the mail. Of course, only Reverend Mother read the letters, but surely she could slit open the envelopes. But no. Reverend Mother trusted her with nothing except to tell her when other nuns weren't keeping the Holy Rule. Perhaps it was enough to be Reverend Mother's eyes and ears, but there were times when Sister Antonetta felt she deserved more.

She took a sip of juice. Had she ever tasted apple juice before? She couldn't remember. It was cold and refreshing, with a sharp taste. She took a biscuit and broke it in half, as she had seen Reverend Mother do many times. It was a plain biscuit, the kind they gave babies. She put one half of it back on the plate and took a bite out of the other half. The plate belonged to the china set that had been given to the convent many years ago by her own family after her mother died. She had not been allowed to go to her mother's funeral, and so, it was very consoling when the china arrived in a big box some-time later. Reverend Mother—the former one—called her into her office and there, on a tray, were two cups and saucers from her mother's set. Reverend Mother poured tea for her, and the two drank tea together from the china cups. From then on, only Reverend Mother and the priest used her mother's china.

She took a longer drink of juice. She noticed, at the top of the desk, a letter opener, gold with a black handle. It gleamed like a miniature sword. She picked up the letter opener and then the white envelope on top of the pile of mail. She slit the envelope open, and the sound, reverberating around the small room, startled her. She took out the contents of the envelope: a letter and a cheque. The letter was folded in thirds. She opened the top flap. "Dear Reverend Mother," she read. She hastily folded it and returned it to the envelope. It wasn't right to read another's letter. The cheque was the colour of a light blue sky. She counted the zeros on it. She had never imagined that amount of money before. She ran her finger along the cheque's surface. Some of the letters were embossed. What luxury it was to hold such a piece of paper, thick with importance, in her hand. She put the cheque in her pocket, placed the envelope on top of the others, and put the letter opener back in its place. She finished off the remaining biscuits and drank the rest of the apple juice. She pushed up the sleeves of her habit and sat back in the comfortable chair. On the wall across from her, beside the bookcase, a framed embroidery piece read, in cross-stitch, "Good example does much good."

Outside the window, she could see the tall hedge and beyond it, the red brick of St. Monica's Girls' School, its windows all parallel to each other like a giant beast with multiple eyes. She herself had been sent for a year of teacher training long ago but had never taught school because of her rheumatic fever. She had lain in bed for months with nothing but plain walls to look at, except for a picture of the Madonna, a matronly Mary holding a naked baby Jesus. She looked at that picture for hours on end, shivering at the nakedness of the Babe.

When she got better, she was given small chores: fetching the morning paper from the front door, bringing in the mail bag. There were moments when she'd watch the school nuns going off to St. Monica's, and if she was outside pulling weeds, she'd hear girls call in friendly voices, "Hello, Sister," to one or another of them. She'd look at the weeds in her hand, their roots shrivelling. Once in a while, when she was still young, she was told to take something to St. Monica's—a package of books, perhaps. What a joy it was to enter the school and see the girls along the wood-lined corridor, dressed in their smart uniforms, their faces fresh and smooth. Once, she was close enough for one of the girls to say, "Good morning, Sister" to her, and she had presumed permission to smile and reply, "Good morning."

When the present Reverend Mother became superior, she had Sister Antonetta doing more chores for her. Most of the things she could do easily, such as bringing up her morning drink. But it had to be said that Reverend Mother was sometimes impatient. One day, the office door became stuck against the floor. The bottom of the door needed to be planed, and Reverend Mother told her to fix it. She had never planed anything before and she asked the superior where she could get the proper implement, whose name she didn't even know. Reverend Mother turned her back and said, "That's your level of generosity, is it?" That rebuke stung, she had to admit.

On Monday of this week, she'd been given the important charge of taking water to St. Monica's, making sure that all the teaching nuns had a drink, and reporting back if any of them broke silence. She felt rather flat, she had to admit, as she watched them standing around in Sister Beatrice's office drinking their water in silence. They then disappeared into their classrooms, leaving her with nothing to report. Then yesterday, Reverend Mother's feast day, the school had been topsy-turvy with excitement and the change in routine, and when she asked Reverend Mother what to do about the nuns' morning drink of water, which they were to take in silence, she'd been waved away with, "Stop talking nonsense. I never heard anything so ridiculous in my life."

She now picked up the tray and left the office. At the end of the corridor, two novices were polishing the floor, the machine making a whirring sound. As she passed the parlour, the door opened and Reverend Mother appeared. Behind her stood the bishop, stooped and silver-haired. Seeing Sister Antonetta and the tray with the empty glass and plate, Reverend Mother's hooded eyes widened. Sister Antonetta bowed to her and stared at the bishop.

"Stay there, Sister," Reverend Mother whispered, indicating the entranceway to the chapel. Sister Antonetta watched as the superior and the bishop walked to the main door. She dearly wanted to make a bolt for the kitchen.

"What are you doing with that tray?" Reverend Mother asked when she returned.

"Mother, I ... wanted to check whether you were in your office and needed your drink."

Reverend Mother picked up the glass and sniffed. "Who drank this?"

Sister Antonetta began to weep. "I'm sorry, Mother. I'm ... sorry for this. I'll..."

She could say no more. She sobbed as she had not done for many a year, struggling to keep the tray upright. Reverend Mother took it from her, and Sister Antonetta took her handkerchief from her pocket and wiped her nose.

Reverend Mother gave the tray back to her and waved Sister Antonetta away. "Go downstairs and wash and dry those things."

Sister Antonetta bowed and said, breathlessly, "Oh, thank you, Mother, thank you." She stumbled to the stairs.

At the entrance to the kitchen, she saw Sister Kate flying about. She took the tray to the sink and began to rinse out the glass and plate. Sister Kate came up behind her, and she froze, then relaxed as the cook said, "Excuse me, Sister," and reached for a pot above the sink.

Sister Antonetta took up the tea towel and dried the glass and plate. After she had put the things back in the brown cupboard, she approached Sister Kate. "May I say just this: Please put the Golden Peel on next week's order." Then she remembered something. "The delivery man said he would bring it. I had permission to ask him. But just to be sure, mark it down."

Sister Kate nodded and smiled. It seemed to be almost a friendly smile. As she left the kitchen, she put her hand in her pocket and felt the embossed lettering of the cheque inside.

9. The Seven Dolours

"WAKEY, WAKEY, RISE AND SHINE, and watch the clouds roll in." That thought had come unbidden as Sister Martha jumped out of bed and gave the response, "Amen," to the sound of the five-thirty a.m. bell. She had lain awake for an hour before that, even though on the face of it, the day ahead promised no clouds. It was Saturday and her charges were few. In-between her usual lesson planning, she would have an extra morning visit to chapel, a few minutes here and there to finish the edging of the table runner that had somehow gotten scorched, and an hour of peeling vegetables in the pantry. In the afternoon, two hours of portress duty.

This last activity happened during all the Saturdays of October. The portress charge gave her a window into a world she had otherwise forgotten existed: Sometimes, men came to the door delivering packages, or mothers came to pick up youngsters from their music lessons and chatted happily without looking over their shoulders. Or when the phone rang, she would answer and take down whatever message would be relayed. A call from Father Such-and-such? "Yes, Father, let me see if Reverend Mother can come to the phone." A birthday call for one of the nuns? "Sister So-and-so isn't available to come to the phone, but thank you, the message will be passed on to her." This kind of phone call was less pleasant for her, because of course, the message would be given to Reverend Mother and she had no idea whether Sister So-and-so would ever receive it.

Well, none of it mattered, because come November, she would be put in charge of polishing the parlour silverware or raking the leaves on Saturday afternoons. Weekend portress duty was given to the teaching nuns who could be trusted to be discreet and to keep the rule of silence. Reverend Mother had placed Sister Martha further in the doghouse, although perhaps, if Sister Martha kept her head down, she might forget. She had a way, Reverend Mother did, of not being predictable, and this could work both ways: Not only could she easily contradict herself—turning a positive into a negative—but she could easily turn a bad mark into not exactly a good mark, but somehow, a non-mark, a nothing.

But the day ahead seemed a not unhappy one. That was how she was feeling as she sat in the chapel, having knelt for the customary five or ten minutes, looking up at the green-curtained tabernacle and the red sanctuary lamp in its gold casing. In her hands, she held a bundle of holy cards Sister Ida had given her a year ago. On the top card, the holier-than-thou nun with the pretty nose and gazing eyes, was St. Rita, just like the life-sized statue that nestled with a group of other statues in Purification Church. You always knew it was St. Rita because of the gash in her forehead, a contrast to the black and white of her religious habit, and a chance for the painter of the picture to dip his brush into some red paint. The gash had come from the crown of thorns that Jesus Himself had supposedly placed on St. Rita's head. Sister Martha turned the card over. "My Beloved, who feedeth among the lilies," the card read. She remembered a retreat priest saying once about the Canticle of Canticles: "You really shouldn't read that book of the Bible unless you know what everything means—that is, what it means in a spiritual sense." Tell me another one, she thought. This was an expression of the students—"Tell me another one!"—always said in a sarcastic voice in response to something unbelievable. Fortunately, so far, she had picked it up only interiorly. She would have to mind her Ps and Qs in order not to let the expression slip out at an untimely moment. It would certainly be seen as vulgar and disrespectful.

Last year, during Sister Martha's stint as the assistant infirmarian, old Sister Ida had been recovering from surgery. The invalid had disregarded the rule of silence entirely, and the two had struck up something close to a friendship. This, of course, would have made Reverend Mother's hair curl, if she had any hair to speak of, but it seemed hardly charitable to rebuff Sister Ida when the old thing wanted to talk.

"In the old days it was different," Sister Ida had said one day as she sat up in bed, her undercap opening to show a wisp of white hair. "We could speak to each other out of charity, and believe me, much charity was needed. Our late Reverend Mother was a saint. She always smoothed things over. Not like…" Her voice trailed, and perhaps she mumbled something, but Sister Martha could make out no more.

Another day, Sister Ida had held in her scrawny fist a small bundle of holy cards held together with an elastic band. "I've got too many of these. Take them." She thrust the cards at Sister Martha. It didn't seem to occur to the old nun that this action only added to Sister Martha's conscience. She should, of course, report to Reverend Mother that Sister Ida had given these holy cards to her without permission. Not to report this would be a violation of the vow of poverty, not only for poor old Sister Ida but also for Sister Martha herself. She should not have held out her hand to accept them, for to do so was to become complicit in the other nun's failure against the vow. She had, of course, not reported her acceptance of the holy cards to Reverend Mother. They sat in her desk dog-eared and brown with years of perspiration from Sister Ida's thumb.

She shifted in the pew now, placing St. Rita's card at the bottom of the bundle and looking down at the face of Christ from the holy Shroud of Turin. Jesus looked dead under a glass case, the marks of the crown of thorns clearly present on His forehead. His eyebrows were dark and His beard white. On the back of the card she read, "I venerate Thy sacred Face whereon there once did shine the beauty and sweetness of the Godhead; but now It has become as it were the face of a leper!" She slipped the card to the back and was now looking at the picture of an all-purpose saint, a man in a shapeless brown garment, with a beard and hair curling around the nape of his neck. On the back, a prayer to St. Jude, the patron saint of lost causes, and in italics, before the prayer itself, instructions: *To be said when one seems to be deprived of all visible help, or for cases despaired of.* Sister Martha looked up at the tabernacle and the flickering sanctuary lamp. This was her prayer: "Most holy apostle St. Jude, faithful servant, whom the Church honours and invokes universally as the patron of hopeless cases, I beseech thee to pray for me who am so miserable...." She smiled. "Pray for me who am so miserable." She might put on a long face and squeaky voice and try this on Sister Kate later, if there were a few moments in the pantry when they could talk: "Sister Kate, pray for me, who am so miserable!"

Her mind turned to the events of the past several days. The rupture in her rapport with the students. What had caused it? The friendly J.J. had become distant; Brooke, beautiful and dull, had begun to cause her no end of trouble. And most of all, Gwen. She hated to admit it, but Gwen's hardness against her was what hurt most of all. The affection of wild things like Gwen was worth more than a thousand Reverend Mothers. She and Sally Sullivan had seen Zélie being carted away, her poor head shamefully exposed. No one knew, of course, what had become of Sister Zélie. What had caused her collapse? Was she still in the hospital? They would have heard if she had died, of course. Indeed, the funeral would have taken place in the convent chapel. She looked down at the holy cards in her hand. A card showing Our Lady of Sorrows was on top, and on the back of the card, the Seven Dolours of Mary. These were Mary's seven moments of sorrow, from the moment Simeon foretold that a sword would pierce her heart, down to the moment when she held the lifeless body of her Son after His crucifixion. What were Sister Martha's own seven dolours? She smiled as she looked at the sanctuary lamp. Here was something to keep her mind occupied as she waited for the bell to ring.

Dolour number one: the genes that gave her a fat body. The habit did nothing to hide it. In fact, it made her look dumpy and comical, as she had noticed one day at the doctor's office where there was a floor-length mirror. Dolour number two: Reverend Mother. Sister Ida had said, if she could be believed, that it didn't have to be like this in religious life. The life of a nun, given up and hidden in Christ, could be flowing over with beneficence and happiness instead of this mere existence of fear from above and ridicule from below. Dolour number three: Sister Beatrice, the Queen Bea. But did she really believe this? Did she really think that the Queen Bea might thwart her, cast her aside? Yes. If there was a choice to be made between the well-being of the teaching nuns and her own ambition—though Sister Martha wasn't sure what that ambition was—then it was clear what action the Queen Bea would take. The teaching nuns could go hurdling down the cliff like the gospel's Gerasene demoniac pigs, no matter how good they might be. She rubbed the soft tops of her fingers with her thumbs and shuddered.

Time to move on. Dolour number four: the students. How could she be so affected by them? The Holy Rule called for a perfect indifference to the suffering of both body and soul. The nun should not care for worldly praise or scorn or condemnation. That equanimity of spirit was the sign of a perfect nun. Why was she so vexed about these girls, especially the ones she used to get along with? She couldn't answer the question.

Dolour number five: God. She sat up straight against the back of the pew and bowed her head. Her neck had become stiff and she tried to relax it by slumping her shoulders. She flexed her feet on the hard kneeler. She would have loved to cross her legs. So God was one of her seven dolours, sending Himself all the way into her heart and soul and body to torment her. Well, God was welcome to her. Beat her to a pulp if He wanted. She was ready to sit back and not bother at all.

Dolour number six: God's will. That was it. It wasn't God Himself who was the problem, it was God's will. How did God's will get decided, and who decided it? She knew perfectly well, of course. It was her superior. And before that, it was God's will that had called her, in the depths of her soul, to the religious life. She'd been glad to leave the farm, not that the farm was bad, but she wanted an education, she wanted to study, and being a nun seemed exciting. She would learn all kinds of important things and then impart them as she stood graceful and elegant and otherworldly in front of a class. The students in front of her would drink from her wisdom. She would be kind but stern when necessary, a model teacher, loved by all. "Sister Martha is my favourite teacher," she would hear repeated up and down the halls. She would smile with indifference—being someone's favourite teacher mattered not at all—and when school was over she would set out with a stately pace, not hurrying, not lagging. She would hold her rosary, praying silently, and she would walk to the chapel, not stopping for any nagging thing. In the chapel, redolent with silence and the faint smell of candle wax, she would close her eyes and drink in the delicious goodness of the surrounding atmosphere—the statues and the dancing vigil lights, the sunshine slanting through the windows, the fragrance of freshly picked flowers on the altar, the sanctuary light indicating that Presence, for Whom she had laid down her life. And, of course, in the centre, there would be Jesus Himself, behind the tabernacle curtain.

What had it come to, this lovely fantasy? There was no an-swer. What was her seventh dolour? The dead pope. Her head shot up. How could she even think such a thing? She quickly slid onto her knees. What a heretical thought that this should even come into her mind. Who was the pope that he should be a dolour on her? Surely she should blame God rather than this poor man. That was all he was, after all—just a man. But even more than Reverend Mother, the pope was the mouthpiece of God. And now he was gone, and the only mouthpiece of God at the moment was Reverend Mother. Heaven help the world if there was no one else to give out God's will except Reverend Mother, with her leathery face and spying underling. A pope shouldn't die and leave the world bereft like that. It meant that life was suspended in the air.

Laughter, quiet but unmistakable, seeped through the pan-try door as Sister Martha approached. As she knocked and entered, the laughter stopped in mid-breath. Sister Kate and Sister Clementia gaped at her, their mouths open. Sister Kate's eyes were watery. She held up a paring knife in one hand and a half-cut onion in the other.

"It's the onions," she said. "Close the door."

"So that's why you're laughing and crying at the same time," Sister Martha said. She looked behind her before closing the door. It was a habit she wasn't happy with—why should she be looking over her shoulder the whole time as if she were some kind of fugitive? She held a potato peeler and had tied back her veil and donned a blue apron.

Sister Martha sniffed the air. "I smell that Lizzie's been here."

"She's just gone. Saturday is her half day."

There was silence as Sister Martha settled herself beside a sack of potatoes. Sister Clementia had already begun peeling.

"What do you think, Sister? Will the bishop do anything?" Sister Kate looked up, blinking away tears as she put the onion down.

"What do you mean? Do anything about what?" It was a mystery how Sister Kate knew everything that was going on, in spite of spending her days in the kitchen, with small periods of respite in the pantry, mostly surrounded by silent novices. Did she have her own spies?

"About Reverend Mother."

"I don't know. What happened?"

"The Queen Bea talked to the extraordinary confessor. About Reverend Mother. And the bishop came to talk to her."

"How do you know this?"

"The Queen Bea said Reverend Mother is going dotty," Sister Clementia said. "Off her head, like." She slapped her hand against her head, making it angle like a rag doll's.

Sister Martha began to laugh. "Well, everyone knows that. What I want to know is why these potatoes are so wrinkly and why this peeler is too dull to get through the skin." She wanted to get the subject off the Queen Bea and Reverend Mother and the bishop. Time enough to get Sister Beatrice by herself next week.

"They're last year's potatoes," Sister Kate said. "You know the rule about holy poverty. Use last year's vegetables first. Don't waste anything."

"Give me a sharp knife, Kate. Yes, I know all about the vow of poverty."

"I remember Reverend Mother in her good days teaching us to peel potatoes." Sister Clementia grinned, her eyes slits behind her thick spectacles, and dropped her hands to her lap. "As if I didn't know how to peel a potato. 'It's for holy poverty,' she says, and she takes the sharpest knife ever you saw and holds up a potato. It was a fresh potato, mind you, just out of the ground, and she slips the peel off, like you skim the cream off the top of milk, and she says, 'That's how you peel a potato.' And she puts the knife in her pocket."

"Leaving the edible part of the potato intact," Sister Martha said. "Holy poverty. Wasting nothing. But let me just cut the peels off, and if parts of the potato come off as well, then poverty be damned." She put her hand over her mouth. "I'm sorry, but..."

"Not to mind, Martha," Sister Kate said. "That potato of Reverend Mother's was partly boiled, I'll bet you that."

The wooden desk in the portress's alcove was small for Sister Martha, but more polished and important-looking than her desk in the common room. The top was covered with a green blotter that had brown leather corners. She felt stupidly grand sitting before that ink blotter, as if she was doing real work, like in a business office downtown. It faced the window, and although there was not much she could see past the iron gate and fence, it pleased her to be reminded that there was a world beyond.

Her planning book, in a three-ring binder, was in front of her, with pieces of loose paper, gathered from over the years, inside the covers. Her pen was scratchy and unsatisfactory today. With a full cartridge it worked well, but the ink was running out. She felt in her pocket for a pencil, and came up with only the tiny one that nestled in her permissions bag. The first Saturday of the month, permissions day, was long over, and she counted on her fingers the number of days she would have to wait till November. What was she going to do for a pen between now and then? If she tried to fiddle with the cartridge, she would get blue ink on her fingers, and if she tried to blow on it to force all the ink to the bottom, the ink would be on her lips and around her mouth. The tiny pencil would have to do.

Beside her planning binder sat the two books she had brought with her to the portress's alcove: the light brown *De Bello Gallico*, which she thought she would try out on her junior Latin class, and *Cicero for Upper Levels*, which might be suitable for some of the clever seniors. Her mind throbbed with thoughts of the Queen Bea and the extraordinary confessor and bishop. Why had Sister Kate brought the matter up, when it was already tucked far back inside her own mind? Why didn't the doorbell ring so that she could be distracted by something from the outside?

She half-heartedly opened *De Bello Gallico*. The Gallic war: the great work of Julius Caesar, and the easiest to translate. She didn't care for translations. She liked teaching Latin grammar, the logical progression from chapter to chapter, the increasing complexity of the language, but with *De Bello Gallico*, she was also expected to regale the students with the exploits of Julius Caesar. The march toward Gaul, the expected fury of the Gallic people, the barbarian hordes, the strategies that had made Julius Caesar such a brilliant general. The new words she'd learned in her own study of Latin and Caesar's military exploits. *Impetus. Battering-ram. Cohort.*

She remembered walking into the classroom one day to see a jingle one of the students had written on the chalkboard: "Latin is a dead language, as dead as dead can be. It killed the ancient Romans, and now it's killing me." They'd had a giggle over that one, she and the girls in the class, in the days—just a few days before—when her rapport with them had been easy, free of tension. But there was something to be said about the jingle. Was Latin killing her as she sat at the portress's desk overlooking the iron fence, where cars drove by, where people walked the street, where the world went on as if nothing else mattered?

She put the book aside and opened *Cicero*. Just inside was a picture of the great orator's bust, his frown evident in the stone. Someone, years before, had coloured his full, downturned lips with a red pen—a student who had somehow got hold of her textbook—and in spite of herself, Sister Martha couldn't help smiling every time she opened the book to that page. Poor old Cicero and his red lips. How the mighty fall into ridicule at the hands of a schoolgirl. But the translation of Cicero was not something to laugh at.

She saw the front gate open. A man dressed in a grey suit began walking up the sidewalk to the front door. An important-looking man, walking with purpose. She held her breath. What was he doing here on a Saturday? He had a white handkerchief in the pocket of his jacket, sticking up about an inch. His hair was darkly silver, and he looked like the kind of aloof man Sister Martha remembered seeing in a bank, aloof and superior. Was he the father of one of the younger nuns? It wasn't likely. As far as she knew, nobody in the community came from the upper classes of society. Except for the Queen Bea, perhaps. But she knew nothing of the principal's background, where she had come from, or where she had gone to school. For all Sister Martha knew, the Queen Bea had sprung, like the ancient goddesses, fully clothed in her perfect nun's habit, from the head, or the feet, or the crotch of Zeus. She blinked and sat up, glad to have something to get her mind off such foolish and uncharitable meanderings.

Anticipating his arrival at the door, she rose from her chair and smoothed down her habit skirt as the man disappeared from her vision and climbed the stairs to the front door. She breathed in deeply and let the breath out slowly at the crisp sound of the doorbell. Then, she unlatched the door. The man had discernible crow's feet, but otherwise his face was unlined and handsome. His eyes were grey-blue, and his nose was straight and slender. As she put on her brightest smile and said what she had been practising for the past few seconds—"Yes, Sir?"—the phone rang.

Immediately, her hand leaped from the door latch to her face, and flustered, she ushered the man into the front parlour, then stood in the foyer, looking backwards and forwards. "I ... phone ... sorry ... phone," she stammered and leaving the front door open, she rushed into the corridor to the telephone room. The man on the other end of the phone didn't identify himself, but said only, "May I speak with your Reverend Mother." Her mind went blank. Was she supposed to ask him his name, or was she to presume he was a person of importance and thus go to fetch Reverend Mother? She had left a man in a grey suit sitting in the front parlour. "It's the bishop speaking," she heard as she was putting the receiver down on the stand.

In the corridor, Sister Clementia was rounding the corner with a mop in her hand. "Clemmie," she whispered. "Go and tell Reverend Mother she's wanted on the phone. It's the bishop! Where is she?"

Her chest heaved as she watched Sister Clementia scurry down the corridor. She turned back to the telephone room and then to the front foyer. How long could she let the bishop dangle on the other end of the telephone? Hearing a flurry of rosary beads, she looked back again and saw Reverend Mother walking at a clip unknown to her before. She made a wide gesture with her right arm to the telephone room, and with her left, she pointed to the foyer, where the important man sat unrecognized and unaddressed in the front parlour. She should at least have steered him to the inside parlour, which had the better furniture. In the front parlour, the cushions didn't match the print of the sofa.

When she reached the foyer, she saw Sister Beatrice closing the front door. The man was smiling at Sister Beatrice and the principal was saying, "Please come to the other parlour." She ignored Sister Martha as she ushered the man away from the front parlour. He was saying, "The extent to which it gets built depends largely upon..." The door of the inside parlour closed behind them.

The Queen Bea was as aware as Sister Martha of the part in the Holy Rule that said, "The Sisters shall never be alone with a person of the opposite sex unless another Sister is present." Did she, as portress, have some responsibility for another's violation of the Holy Rule? Should she, in charity, tell Reverend Mother, after the phone call with the bishop was over, that Sister Beatrice was in the parlour with a man? Of course: To not do so was to overlook a duty in charity.

She was still standing between the foyer and the corridor when Reverend Mother emerged from the telephone room. "Mother..." she began.

"Who was at the door?" Reverend Mother's hooded eyes had opened wide.

"It was a man, Mother. He didn't say. The phone rang just as..."

"Where is he, then? What did you do with him?"

"He's in the good parlour, Mother. Sister Beatrice is..."

"Off with you. Why are you standing in the doorway?" Reverend Mother waved her away and moved down the corridor to the other parlour. She opened the door and disappeared inside, closing the door behind her.

Sister Martha returned to the portress's desk. She opened the book of *Cicero* to the page with the red-lipped bust. With her scratchy pen, she began to draw round blue circles inside the blanks of the eyes.

10. Sweet Music

S ISTER BEATRICE STOPPED IN FRONT of the school bulletin board, and catching her breath, took a step backward and stared at it. The homeroom bell had sounded five minutes earlier, and the girls had gone helter-skelter to class, arms full of books and binders, maroon skirts swinging. She had started her usual walk along the corridor to the front door, clearing her mind of other matters, recalling her morning meditation. Today, the meditation had been about the woman at the well, to whom Jesus says, "Give me some of your water." And the woman gapes at him in disbelief.

She herself now gaped. She had stopped to survey the bulletin board, making sure there were no out of date posters or untidy notices. A full-page advertisement had been torn out of a magazine and roughly, perhaps hurriedly, tacked up on the board, right under the sign that declared, "Nothing is to be placed on the bulletin board without the principal's permission." The picture featured a young woman who wore a long flowing skirt and pointy heels, and on top, nothing but a brassiere. Behind her floated a sheet of music. The heading of the advertisement read, "I dreamed I made sweet music in my Maidenform bra." The woman's face was beautiful and fine-boned, with a slight cleft in her chin. Her hair was short and dark.

Someone had scrawled at the top of the page, "Brooke Hankey made ugly music in her..." She pulled out the tacks that had fastened the picture and took it down. The young woman did look like Brooke, but more importantly, the picture had been tacked onto the bulletin board to ridicule the girl in the most tawdry and uncharitable way. By a St. Monica's girl. Because she, Sister Beatrice, had favoured Brooke over Sally Sullivan at Reverend Mother's feast day concert. But what choice did she have? The doctor's daughter or the daughter of a generous millionaire? And what to do now about this serious infraction?

When she got back to her office, the telephone was ringing. She placed the picture on her desk as she picked up the receiver.

"Sister Beatrice?" The male voice was familiar, but he didn't immediately identify himself. "I wonder if I might come by. I've been at the hospital and thought I'd swing around and have a word with you."

"You are...?" Then she remembered whom the voice belonged to. "Father Doyle! Oh, yes, do come by. You'll be here when? In ten minutes? Yes, of course."

She looked around the office after she hung up the receiver. What did Father Doyle want? There were only the two straight-backed chairs facing the principal's desk, and these would have to do if he wanted to talk. But she would have to offer him something to drink. Did he drink coffee or tea at this time of the day? How could she get it for him on such short notice? There was nothing for it but to presume permission—that dreaded option—and head over to the convent for a tray.

Inside the convent, approaching the kitchen, she heard the murmur of voices coming from the pantry. She knocked on the pantry door and entered.

"It's the state of the world that has me worried," Lizzie was saying. She sat at the table with a thick mug of tea in front of her and a half-smoked cigarette between two fingers. Sister Kate was cutting the tops and tails of green and yellow beans with a pair of scissors, and Sister Clementia, sitting beside her, was slicing them into a large pot.

Seeing Sister Beatrice at the door, Lizzie said, "Do the Russians not worry you, Sister?"

"The Russians?" Sister Beatrice paused, looking from one to the other of the two nuns. "Is it … can you … I have permission … a priest is coming to the school. Now. Can you make a pot of coffee or tea?"

Sister Kate put her scissors down. "Coffee or tea is it, Sister? Right now? I'm behind with the vegetables. That's why Sister Clementia…"

"Whichever is quickest. He just phoned now to let me know he was coming." As the cook rose, Sister Beatrice added, "Thank you for your charity, Sister Kate." She felt breathless, and her palms were wet. She surreptitiously rubbed them against her habit skirt.

"They'll be after the Catholics first," Lizzie said. "That's what Father said on Sunday. He said they want to kill all the priests in the world, or maybe send them into outer space in that rocket ship they call the Sputnik."

Sister Beatrice looked over at Sister Clementia, who didn't raise her head from slicing the beans. She surveyed the tins in the shelves overhead. "Perhaps a nice biscuit from one of those tins," she said aloud.

Sister Kate burst into the pantry. "I put the kettle on for tea, Sister. That will be the fastest thing."

"And make it a nice tray. With the best china…"

"Sister, what do you think? I'm going to set a tray for a priest as if he's a workman?"

"I'm sorry, I'm just flustered by the…"

"Sister Beatrice." It was Lizzie again. "Is it true about the Russians?"

Sister Beatrice kept her eye on the cook's movements. "A biscuit from one of those tins," she whispered. Sister Kate took a tin down from the shelf and disappeared again into the kitchen.

"That's what Father said, Sister," Lizzie continued. "If those Russians ... "

"The Russians aren't all Communists, Lizzie. It's the Communists..."

"Yes, the *Communists*. That's what they are. They don't even believe in God. They want to kill the priests."

Sister Kate reappeared with a tea tray. Sister Beatrice took a quick appraisal. All was as it should be. She took the tray from the cook.

Sister Kate returned to her chair. As Sister Beatrice was closing the door behind her, she saw the cook holding the scissors aloft like a sword. "If the Russians come over here, keep your scissors close by, Lizzie," Sister Kate said. "Cut their throats, like." Then she laughed.

When Sister Beatrice reached the principal's office with the tea tray, Father Doyle was standing beside her desk with the page ripped from the magazine in his hand.

"Some interesting material," he said. "I gather not allowed? Taken down by the principal from the bulletin board?"

Sister Beatrice didn't answer. She looked about for a place to set the tray. There was nothing else in the room but the two chairs facing the principal's desk. She pushed aside some papers on the desk and set the tray down and indicated one of the chairs. "Please sit down, Father," she said. She suppressed the urge to apologize for the lack of suitable furniture in the office. That was something to consider for another time. She thought she might sit in the principal's chair, on the other side of the desk, but such a move would emphasize her role as principal, her superiority to her visitor, and such a position would not be suitable when a priest was the visitor. She sat on the chair beside him. She immediately rose again to pour the tea. "A cup of tea, Father?"

Father Doyle shook his head. "I'm a coffee man, thanks. Tea is for nuns."

Again, she thought of replying, but decided to ignore the comment. Better to stay pleasant. Neutral. She didn't know what the priest wanted, but he was the one she had spoken to in confidence, and he held the key to improving the precarious situation in her life. She held out a napkin and a plate of buttered toast and biscuits. "Some toast?"

He backed away in his chair and held up his hands, as if to push away the plate. It took Sister Beatrice a few seconds to realize he was declining. She put the napkin and the plate on the tray and sat back.

The priest reached over and set the ripped page back on the desk. Sister Beatrice felt her face redden as, out of the corner of her eye, she looked at the picture of the woman in the brassiere. She wanted to reach out and turn it over. Why hadn't she thrown it away immediately? Did she really want to show it around to the girls, to risk laughter and ridicule, to embarrass Brooke, just to find out the identity of the culprit? What else had she thought to do with the page?

Father Doyle shifted and crossed his legs. His black suit was impeccable. He had, after all, been visiting the hospital, perhaps had attended to a dying person. "I've spoken to the bishop," he began. Sister Beatrice held her breath. Surely he wasn't about to discuss in plain daylight, in her office, what she had talked about in the hushed darkness of the confessional, or was he? "We thought St. Monica's could do with a chaplain," he said.

Sister Beatrice let out her breath and her shoulders dropped. She didn't realize how tense she'd become. Still, this was an unexpected statement, a side thrust. What was she supposed to answer? "The bishop thought this?" She posed it as a question, playing for time. "We do have the priests from Purification Church," she began slowly. "They come here from time to time to speak to the girls."

"From time to time, but not on a regular basis." It was a flat statement. His eyes were back on the picture of the woman in the brassiere.

"What did you have in mind, Father?"

"Some regular talks. Go to each of the classes in turn."

"Each of the classes? You would come here every day, then?"

"We'd work it out. Whenever it would suit the school's schedule."

"It would be good to have a priest here every day, that's true. Especially if the bishop wants it. To help the girls with their spiritual problems. To hear confession on a regular basis. Would you help to teach the religion classes?"

"You bet I would. Isn't that what I'm here for?"

"It would be a change from hearing the nuns talking all the time. The girls need to hear from a priest more often, away from a church setting."

The priest was silent for a moment, and then said, "And sports. I could help with sports."

"How do you mean, Father?"

"I could coach the girls' basketball team."

"Coach?"

"I coached St. Paul's boys' basketball team while I was in the seminary." He raised his fist to his mouth as if blowing a whistle or a trumpet. "I'm a pro at coaching."

"Reverend Mother will be pleased. If the bishop would like it..." She stopped herself, realizing she had made a direct reference to Reverend Mother. Should she say something about the letter she had written to him? About her confession? About whether or not he had spoken to the bishop?

He picked up the page again from the desk. Now he was the one who seemed to redden. "'Brooke Hankey made ugly music'?" He had a puzzled frown on his face. "Hankey. Is she the daughter of...?"

She nodded, and he widened his eyes. "Oh boy, you've got some little bitches here," he said.

She drew in her breath. She had never heard a priest use such language before.

"A dangerous species. Some of them, anyway." He smiled.

"It's a sewer out there, Sister. You don't know the half of it. It'll be good to have me around, to teach something to these girls."

"You say 'some of them,' Father."

"Oh, listen, I hear confessions. I know what goes on out there."

"We have basically good girls in St. Monica's, Father. They're lively, of course, and we really try our best...."

The bell rang for the change of class, and the priest jumped up, threw the page back on the desk. At the door of the office, he turned. "The conclave in Rome starts this weekend. The guessing game is on."

Sister Beatrice looked blankly at him. She had forgotten that a new pope would soon be elected. "Oh yes," she said.

At the back entrance to the convent, with the untouched tray in her hands, Sister Beatrice saw Reverend Mother rounding the corner to the nuns' refectory. Sister Antonetta was at her heels, and she looked up in surprise at Sister Beatrice. There was nothing else to do but to put on a dignified, businesslike expression, the one that frightened the girls. Some of them, anyway. Did she ever think she'd be at Sister Antonetta's mercy? She was inside two worlds: the world of priests who knew everyone's secrets, and the world of the convent spy system.

As she passed the refectory door, Sister Antonetta gave her a suspicious look and Sister Beatrice bowed solemnly and held up the tray toward Reverend Mother's back, holding her breath lest the superior should look around. She then bowed again to Sister Antonetta, hoping the other saw in her a combination of humility and confidence, the look of a nun who was above reproach.

At the entrance to the kitchen, Sister Kate was putting the pot of beans onto the stove. A novice was bent over the far sink, scrubbing something. There were ears underneath that white, well-starched coif. Sister Beatrice set the tray down on a sideboard. "He didn't want any," she whispered. "Can Lizzie eat this?" Then looking up at the ceiling, she added, "No need to mention anything upstairs."

Sister Kate looked around at the novice. She said nothing.

"You know what I mean?" Sister Beatrice whispered.

"That's right, Sister," Sister Kate replied, then jerked her head at the pantry. "There's more vegetables needed." She now motioned with her hand, and Sister Beatrice followed her.

In the pantry, Sister Kate said "What happened with Reverend Mother and the bishop?"

Sister Beatrice looked at her blankly.

"She met with him upstairs," Sister Kate said. "Last week."

"Last week? Upstairs?" She felt stupid. Why hadn't Father Doyle told her? But of course, why would Father Doyle have said anything? It would be like breaking the seal of the confessional.

"We may see some changes. That's what someone said."

"Sister Kate, I have to be getting back. The priest said he doesn't drink tea. He wouldn't have any toast or biscuits. He's keeping his girlish figure."

"Does Reverend Mother know you talked with Father Doyle?"

"Who said I talked with Father Doyle?"

"Wasn't that him then?"

"It was school business, Sister."

"Then, you weren't talking to him about Reverend Mother?"

"No."

Sister Kate turned to leave, and Sister Beatrice said, "You won't tell her, will you? You'll get rid of that tray right away, give the food to Lizzie? Does she come over here for her lunch?"

"So you didn't speak to Father Doyle about Reverend Mother?"

Sister Beatrice hesitated, and then said, "Yes, that's right."

The bell signalling the end of the school day had rung, and as always, the hallway filled with commotion, chairs scraping the floor inside classrooms, girls calling out, pushing, pulling. Doors opening and closing, voices chattering. She had thought she might walk up and down among them as they drifted around her, talking, chatting, saying "Goodbye Sister" and "See you tomorrow Sister." She would hold the brassiere advertisement and the ugly scrawl prominently as she walked. In fact, she had practised walking with it in her hands, back and forth in the office, trying to make the page both conspicuous and inconspicuous, so that the innocent girls wouldn't notice, but the guilty ones would become evident by the looks on their faces. She would then note who these girls were and would talk to them tomorrow.

This plan didn't happen. She had sat down at her desk and had tried to concentrate on paperwork, but had thought instead of Father Doyle and Reverend Mother. Looking at the black phone in front of her. Wondering whom she might call. Was there someone out there she might call to talk over her problems with? Even if there were, would she dare?

She now smiled her goodbyes in the hallway as the page with the advertisement and the scrawl sat on her desk. At the far end of the hallway, she saw Sally Sullivan with another girl she didn't know well. The girl's name, she seemed to remember, was Gwen. She walked with purpose over to them.

Sally was buttoning her jacket over her uniform, her books and binder sprawled on the floor. As she bent to pick them up, she saw Sister Beatrice approaching. Gwen was leaning against the wall just inside the front door with a glum expression on her face.

"Girls, may I talk to you a moment?"

Sally straightened and smiled. Gwen slowly dislodged herself from the wall. Neither spoke.

"What are you doing now? Are you going to meet with some of your friends?" The questions seemed to come from nowhere.

"We're going to Betty's, Sister," Sally said. She seemed pleasant enough, didn't carry a grudge.

"Betty's? Who's Betty?"

"That's the coffee shop. We'll likely get a Coke or a milk-shake. Meet..."

"Oh, I see. Of course, that's where the boys from St. Paul's go."

The girls shifted their feet. The three of them standing there in the hallway, it seemed as if an interview was being conducted, but was going nowhere. She didn't like the feeling of standing still, a conversation drawn to a halt. It was time to come to the point. "Did either of you girls put up a sign on the bulletin board without permission?"

Both girls looked blank.

She looked from one to the other. "This morning, or yesterday after school?"

"No, Sister," Sally said.

"A sign, Sister?" Gwen said.

"Yes, it was an advertisement from a magazine, and it said some hateful things about one of the other girls in the school."

"An advertisement, Sister?" Was Sally being disingenuous? Was she laughing at her, hoping that Sister Beatrice would describe the advertisement and the scrawl to them?

She made a gesture with her hand down to the floor. "It showed a woman..." She could say no more. "Someone wrote things on it about one of the girls. I thought one of you might know about it."

The girls shook their heads. It was difficult to know as she watched them burst through the front door into freedom, whether one or another of them was the guilty party or not.

As she hoped, Sister Martha was still in her homeroom after all the girls had gone. She was by the window, a favourite perch, when Sister Beatrice entered. As she had been doing recently, she was working some white edging onto a piece of needlework.

Sister Beatrice held out the picture of the woman in the brassiere. "See what one of our beauties has been doing? Do they have nothing else to do? No Latin homework?" She felt the need to show another nun the transgression, but she also wanted to make light of it. She had already decided she didn't want to confront any of the girls who were possibly guilty.

"Just a minute." Sister Martha took a pair of scissors out of a scabbard and snipped the thread close to the cloth. "Finished." She held up the cloth for Sister Beatrice's inspection. "It's wrinkled, but some starch and ironing will make it like new again." Her expression changed to one of puzzlement as she took the picture from Sister Beatrice's outstretched hand. "What's this?"

Sister Beatrice said nothing, waiting for her reaction.

Sister Martha looked at her, still puzzled. "Where did you find this?"

"The bulletin board. No permission from me, I needn't tell you."

"Who do you think did it?"

"Someone who doesn't like Brooke, I suppose, who wasn't happy that Brooke sang at last week's concert and that Sally didn't." Sister Beatrice shrugged.

"What are you going to do about it?"

Sister Beatrice stifled a yawn. "I wish I had simpler things to think about, like laundering and starching a nice piece of cutwork."

"That's the least of my troubles, believe me." Sister Martha folded the runner and reached for her work-bag.

"What do you mean by that?"

"Today wasn't so bad, but the classes haven't been going so well lately. We're getting into some pure translation, and I don't know, but there's a different tone in one or two of the classes. I can't quite put my finger on it." She gave a slow smile. "Who was the cute priest?"

"What? *Cute* priest?"

"One of the girls went to the washroom, and after class I heard her saying, 'Sister Beatrice has a cute priest in her office.'"

"They don't miss a thing do they?" Sister Beatrice looked to the door. She lowered her voice. "It was Father Doyle. He wants to become the school chaplain. The bishop approves, and he'll also coach St. Monica's basketball team."

Sister Martha's mouth hung open. Sister Beatrice smiled. "Are you trying to catch a fly?"

"Just make sure the uniforms are modest."

"Modest? Of course they're modest. Besides, if the bishop approves of having Father Doyle coach the basketball team, who are you to disapprove?"

Sister Martha swung her work-bag back and forth. "You're right. Who am I to disapprove?"

It was better to get back to the matter at hand. "I tried talking with two of the girls a few minutes ago. Sally Sullivan. I'm sure you remember that I had to cut her out of the concert because that…" She stopped and then continued: "I was going to give her a bad name. I'll call her Brooke, out of charity—because Brooke wanted to sing her song instead. The other girl's name is Gwen."

Sister Martha's eyebrows lifted slightly. "What did they say?"

"They said they knew nothing. They may know more than they're letting on. I can do no more." She glanced at the picture. "My experience tells me that slights may not be forgotten. A grudge may be long-lasting. But revolutions don't happen because of bulletin board notices that a principal catches before any real harm is done. If Brooke had seen it, I'd be hearing from her father right now. The phone isn't ringing. All is well."

She tore the picture in two, then looked at the bottom half. "It's a very pretty skirt, though. And if she was covered up on top, it would be a beautiful picture." She continued tearing it into pieces.

11. Whiter Than Snow

S ALLY AND J.J. SAT SIDE BY SIDE in the farthest booth in Betty's Coffee Shop, with Gwen facing them across the table. Glasses of Coke stood in front of all three, and in the centre, a plate of French fries. Sally and J.J. had shrugged off their jackets and both had their arms folded on top of the table, their uniform sleeves rolled up to their elbows. Gwen wore a light brown suede jacket with fringes on the sleeves over her uniform. She picked up a long, thin fry and dangled it over the formica table, then let it drop.

"How long did you say it's been?" Sally asked.

"I don't know," Gwen said. "I don't really keep track. But it's been a long time. I'm pretty sure."

"Did you go all the way with...?"

J.J. gave Sally a scornful look. "She *must* have if she thinks..."

Gwen turned her glass around one way and then the other. Her fingernails were bitten to the quick.

"My father's a doctor..." Sally began.

Gwen's eyes flashed with anger. "I *know* your father's a doctor."

Sally blushed. "I just mean, you need a doctor to tell you one way or the other. Maybe there's nothing to worry about. But honestly, Gwen, you shouldn't..."

"Don't tell her what to do," J.J. cut in. "Well, except, Gwen, you *do* need to see a doctor. But it doesn't have to be Dr. Sullivan."

Gwen slumped back in her seat. "I guess I should. Can you make an appointment with your father for me?"

Sally picked up a French fry and took a small bite. "That's not the way it works."

"What do you mean?"

"You have to make your own appointments."

J.J. turned to Sally. "Come on, can't you help her out? Gwen's a friend."

Sally pulled at her straw.

"Your dad can help her, can't he?"

"Yes, but...." Sally took a sip of her Coke.

Gwen sat up. "She doesn't want her dad to know she has a friend who does that sort of thing." She faced Sally. "Your friends have to be squeaky clean. Isn't that it?"

"Pure as the driven snow," J.J. murmured.

Sally squirmed in her seat. "It's not exactly that."

"What is it, then?" J.J. said.

"Well, so what? If you've got yourself into trouble, whose fault is that? It's a mortal sin, and you'll have to go to confession...."

J.J. poked Sally with her elbow. "Sally, just shut up, will you?"

Gwen's lips tightened. Sally curled her fingers around her glass, her eyes downcast.

J.J turned back to Gwen. "Anyway, Gwen, you need to talk to somebody. An adult."

Sally brightened. "Maybe Sister Martha."

Gwen looked at her. "Are you kidding? Sister Marshmallow?"

"Well, how about Sister Zélie then?" Sally said. "She's young. She'd understand."

"She's also French," J.J. said. "French people know about these things."

Gwen frowned. "About what things?"

"About sex and all that. Maybe she even..."

"J.J.!" Sally slapped J.J.'s shoulder. "Watch your language!"

"All I'm saying is that Sister Zélie is the sort of nun you can probably talk to. She's strict, but she's also understanding. Remember that time she caught you cheating?"

Sally turned sharply.

"Come on, I saw you," J.J. said. "You had your textbook hidden inside your desk, and Sister Zélie come up from behind. She whispered something to you, but she didn't say anything in front of the class."

Gwen looked at Sally with interest.

Sally ran her finger around the bottom of her glass. After a moment, she said, "She took marks off, but she didn't tell Sister Beatrice. She said, 'It's between you and me, and we'll just forget about it.'"

J.J. said to Gwen, "See? She's not going to tell you that you're a sinner. She'll help you. She should be back from the hospital by now. Her operation was a couple of weeks ago."

Gwen sat up. "I never thought of talking to one of the nuns. But Sister Zélie's pretty good."

Sally looked past the booths and over to the restaurant's entrance. "Oh boy, look who's here."

J.J. followed her gaze and put her hand up to her mouth. She looked across at Gwen, who had slumped back in her seat.

"Should we pretend we don't see them?" J.J. said.

Before either girl could answer, two St. Paul's boys arrived at the booth, both wearing the school's navy blazer and grey pants, their shirts open at the throat.

"Look who the cat dragged in." Sally pushed against J.J. to make room for one of the boys. Gwen, blinking as if aroused from sleep, followed suit and slid over, dragging her glass along the tabletop.

"Hi, Kevin. Hi, Bob," J.J. said. There was irritation in her voice.

Sally smiled at them. "What brings you two here?"

"What brings anybody here?" Kevin said. He leaned over to Gwen and winked at the two girls across the table. Gwen shrank away from him.

The waitress appeared, and the two boys ordered Cokes.

"What's up?" Bob helped himself to a French fry.

"Nothing much," Sally smoothed her hair and wrinkled her nose at him.

"Why weren't you girls at the game today?" Bob opened his hand to reveal his crumpled navy-and-white striped school tie. He stretched it out and began to twirl it. "The St. Monica's cheerleaders were there, and they said the nuns gave you the last period off. Friday afternoon, time off to cheer on the good Catholic boys over at St. Paul's."

"Yeah, a lot of the girls were there," Kevin said. He stood up, extended his arms and in a clumsy dancing gyration, sang, "*Oh, when the Saints go marching in! Oh, when the Saints...*" His jacket collar bounced as he sang.

The waitress arrived with their Cokes, and he sat down again. "No, seriously, they're impressive, those cheerleaders. Can they ever kick!"

"You girls missed the game of the season," Bob said. "Duggan made three touchdowns."

"We're gonna be the best team in the league this year," Bob said to Kevin across the table. "Better guys in the defensive backfield."

"Duggan's a strategist. And a better quarterback than we had last year."

Sally picked up Bob's school tie. She put it around her neck, flipping one end over the other. "How do you do this?"

"Do what?" Kevin reached across and pulled down one end of the tie.

"Tie a tie." Sally turned to Bob. He took hold of the tie, and Sally ran a finger along his hand as he flipped the tie over, under, and into a knot. His hand lingered.

"Watch it, Mister," Sally said. "Untouchable." She smiled across the table.

"What? What?" Bob raised his eyebrows in mock-innocence and picked up his glass.

"And Peterson! Those three passes he intercepted," Kevin said. "He's a pretty good runner too."

"Who cares about football?" Gwen shifted in her seat. She turned away from him toward the wall, then said, "Excuse me, I want out of here."

"What's with you?" Kevin turned to face her. "How come you weren't...?"

"Let her out, Kevin," J.J. cut in.

His jaw dropped at the sharpness in J.J.'s voice, and he slid out to give Gwen room to leave.

"See you later, Gwen," J.J. called. "Gwen?"

Gwen disappeared out the restaurant door without looking back.

"What's wrong with her?" Kevin slid back into his seat.

"Should I go with her?" J.J. whispered to Sally.

Sally shook her head. She fingered the knot at her throat. "I like school ties," she said.

The doorbell had rung twice on Saturday morning by the time Sister Antonetta reached the foyer. When she opened the door, Gwen was poised to ring it a third time.

"Yes," Sister Antonetta said.

Gwen stood squarely in the doorway as if she was afraid the old nun would shut the door in her face. She looked pale and drawn and her hair was dishevelled. She held an envelope in her hand. "Is Sister Zélie here?" There was a note of defiance in her voice.

Sister Antonetta drew herself up straight. "I beg your pardon."

Gwen shifted her feet. "I heard she's back from the hospital."

"May I ask if that is any business of yours?" Sister Antonetta looked her up and down, and her eyes remained fixed on the girl's brown skirt, short white socks, and brown loafers. "Are you one of the girls that come for Sister Estelle's Saturday music lessons?"

"No. I came to see Sister Zélie."

"Sister Zélie cannot receive visitors."

"Why not?"

"My dear child, we have a Rule. The only visitors we can see are our own families, twice a year." She looked more closely at Gwen. "How do you know Sister Zélie? You're not a St. Monica's girl, are you?"

"Yeah, I am."

"I should think a St. Monica's girl would be rather more polite than..."

Gwen held out the envelope. "Will you give her a letter for me?"

The nun looked at the envelope with suspicion and slowly took it from the girl.

"You'll see that she gets it, please? And can you tell her hi from me? I'm Gwen. I'm in her French class, and I hope to see her soon." She turned to leave.

"Very well." Sister Antonetta watched as the girl descended the steps. She closed the door and hastened down the corridor to Reverend Mother's office.

"Yes?" came a voice in response to the nun's knock.

Sister Antonetta opened the door and stepped inside. "Mother, a girl came to the door just now and wanted to see Sister Zélie. She gave me this." She handed the envelope to the superior. "She looked rather disreputable, if I may say so, Mother."

Reverend Mother stood at her desk. A magazine with coloured photos was open before her. She waved the envelope in the air in an absent-minded gesture. "Look at them, they're magnificent."

Sister Antonetta leaned over the desk. Spread across both pages were portraits of cardinals in their red taffeta robes and lace surplices, some wearing red birettas, others holding their scarlet, wide-brimmed hats.

"The conclave begins today," Reverend Mother said. "Right now, the cardinals are inside the Sistine Chapel, voting on who will be the next Holy Father." She waved the envelope over the magazine. "It may be any one of these men. The Holy Spirit will guide them, I feel sure." She looked at the envelope, a slight expression of surprise on her face, as if she didn't know she was holding it. She reached for the letter opener on her desk and slit it open. She unfolded the letter while Sister Antonetta craned her neck to look at the cardinals' pictures.

Reverend Mother read the letter silently:

Dear Sister Zélie,
I hope you are feeling better. I said the rosary for you.
May I come to see you soon? I have something to ask
you about. It is very serious. I have to talk to somebody.
Please let me know when I can come to see you. You
can phone me.

The girl had written her phone number and signed the letter, "Love Gwen," followed by a series of Xs and Os.

Reverend Mother folded the letter, returned it to the envelope, and tore it into several small pieces. She held her arm over the wastebasket and dropped them in.

Lizzie was sitting across from Sister Kate in the pantry and smoking a cigarette when the door crept open and Sister Antonetta's head appeared.

"What are you doing here?" Sister Antonetta asked, entering and sniffing the smoke.

"Having me morning fag, Sister, and a chat with Sister Kate before I head home. It's me half day."

Sister Antonetta turned to Sister Kate. "You shouldn't be having a *chat*, as she calls it, with anybody."

Sister Kate smiled. "Right, Sister. Silence it is."

For a moment, the only sound was the soft *whish* coming from Lizzie's mouth as she blew smoke into the air. Pipes rattled from the vicinity of the kitchen. Sister Antonetta shifted her feet and said, "I came to get Reverend Mother's morning drink."

"As you like, Sister," Sister Kate said.

"And a sweet biscuit. Not those plain biscuits."

"That's fine, Sister. Reverend Mother likes those rich tea biscuits." Sister Kate reached for a brightly coloured biscuit tin on a shelf above the loaves of bread. She arranged two biscuits on a plate, then replaced the tin on the shelf. "I'll get a glass from the kitchen."

When she had gone, Sister Antonetta said to Lizzie, "She gets to have everything, and the rest of us get nothing."

"D'you not have a drink of something in the middle of the morning, Sister? Not a cup of tea?"

"I don't get the things I need. She doesn't let me."

"Will Reverend Mother not let you have a biscuit like herself?"

"Oh my land, no. Those sweet biscuits are only for her. They cost a lot of money. It would be against the vow of poverty if we were to all have them every day. With Reverend Mother, now, that's different. She's the superior and takes the place of Christ. She deserves the best. Still and all, you'd think she'd want to share with us once in a while. You don't see *her* observing the vow of poverty very much." She put a finger to her lips. "Hush now, I shouldn't be saying this."

Sister Kate returned with a glass of juice. She placed the glass on the tray and held the tray out to Sister Antonetta. The other nun didn't move.

"Is there something else, Sister?" Sister Kate asked.

"Can't you offer me something? Why do the lay people get all the privileges?"

"What do you mean, Sister?"

Sister Antonetta pointed to the mug of tea in front of Lizzie. "She gets that every morning. She probably had a sweet biscuit too."

"No, Sister, just me fag." Lizzie held up her cigarette.

Sister Kate reached once again for the tin on the top shelf. Opening it, she said, "Sister, I think Reverend Mother might like to have *three* sweet biscuits this morning. Why don't you take another one?" She winked at Lizzie as Sister Antonetta took a cookie from the tin and slipped it into her pocket.

Sally and J.J. were already in Betty's Coffee Shop when Gwen arrived on Saturday afternoon. They were both dressed in pullover sweaters and pleated skirts and were drinking milkshakes. As Gwen slipped into the booth beside Sally, she grabbed the other girl's milkshake and took a long drag on the straw.

"Wow!" Sally said. "Haven't you had anything to eat today?"

Gwen swallowed the last bit of milkshake and wiped her mouth. She shook her head.

"Where have you been all day?" J.J. asked.

"I went to the convent to see Sister Zélie, but that old nun wouldn't let me see her. I left her a letter."

"What did you say in the letter?" Sally asked.

"I said I needed to talk to her."

"That's good," Sally said. "That way, if the old nun reads it first, she won't know what it's about."

"Why would she do that?" J.J. took a sip of her milkshake. "You're not supposed to read other people's letters, even if you're a crotchety old nun."

"Oh, but the Reverend Mother reads all the nuns' letters," Sally said. "My dad said so."

Gwen frowned. "How does your dad know that?"

Sally shrugged. "People tell him things."

"Well, even if she does read my letter to Sister Zélie, there's nothing in it except that I want to talk to her. That's not a crime, is it?"

The girls were silent for a moment, and then J.J. said, "Who is it, Gwen?"

"Who is what?"

"Who's the guy?"

Gwen fidgeted and looked around for the waitress. "Can I borrow some money? I want to get a hamburger."

"Sure, go ahead," Sally said. "You don't want to tell us?"

"What if I did? I don't even know if I *am* yet."

There was another moment's silence. The waitress arrived, and Gwen ordered a hamburger. Then Sally spoke: "I asked my father last night how you know when you're pregnant. I didn't say "pregnant,' because I'm not supposed to know that word. I said, 'when you're going to have a baby.'"

"What did he say?" Gwen asked.

"After he came down from the ceiling, he said, 'Do you know a girl who's this way?' Maybe he thought I was asking for myself. I lied and said that we needed to know it for our biology class."

J.J. snorted. "That's a laugh. How can the nuns teach it when they don't know anything about it themselves?"

"I think they're just not allowed to," Sally said. "It's their Holy Rule or something. That's what my father said."

J.J. leaned over to Gwen. "What are you going to do, Gwen? You can't hang around waiting for Sister Zélie to answer your letter."

Gwen pointed to the phone booth outside the door of the coffee shop. "I'm giving that old nun time to give her my letter, then I'm going to phone her."

"The first thing you have to find out is whether you *are* or not," J.J. said. "You should see a doctor on Monday."

"I've heard there are things you can do to..." Gwen said.

Sally's eyes widened. "Don't say such a thing!"

"Like what?" J.J. asked.

"You can sit in a hot bath. Or ride horseback."

Sally rolled her eyes. "Where are you going to find a horse?"

"I've heard you can drink something like bleach or bluing." Gwen lowered her voice. "That's what prostitutes do."

"Bleach'll kill you. If you are—you know—if you *are*, there are places you can go," J.J. said, spreading her hands on the table. "A doctor can arrange for you to go somewhere, have the baby, and then give it away."

Gwen put her head down on the table. "I wish I knew what to do," she said, her voice muffled by her sleeve.

J.J. leaned over and touched her arm. "Sister Zélie probably has your letter by now. Why don't you phone her?"

Gwen slid out of the booth and walked to the door, her gait somewhat unsteady. The other two watched as she put a coin into the slot of the pay phone and held the receiver tightly to her ear. When she returned a few minutes later, a hamburger was on the table at her place. She squeezed ketchup on it and took a bite.

"So?" Sally said.

Gwen swallowed. "Sister Martha answered the phone." She wiped ketchup from the corner of her mouth with her finger. "At least it wasn't the old nun I gave the letter to. I told her I wanted to talk to Sister Zélie. She didn't say anything, so I said it again, and she said, 'We can't talk on the phone.'"

J.J. frowned. "Is that all she said?"

"She said, 'Gwen, the nuns aren't allowed to have personal phone calls.' Then she kind of whispered, 'Is anything wrong?' I could hardly hear her."

"And?" Sally said.

"And I didn't know what to say, so I hung up."

On Sunday morning, Sister Martha and Sister Estelle made the short walk to Purification Church for the ten o'clock Mass. It was the last Sunday of the month, the Sunday on which St. Monica's school choir sang at Mass. As they were entering the church, Sister Martha spied Gwen sitting on the fence next door. She whispered to the other nun, "I'm going over to that girl."

Sister Estelle looked around at the people making their way into the church and whispered, "It'll get back to Reverend Mother. We're to speak to the choir girls only, and only about deportment and music."

"Gwen's in some kind of trouble," Sister Martha said. "Reverend Mother can do what she likes about it."

As she walked over to the fence, a large black car pulled up to the curb. A man with steel-grey hair emerged from the passenger side and opened the back door. A woman in a navy blue hat with a net veil got out, and behind her came Brooke Hankey, whose trim black velvet hat blended into her hair. She wore a bright red coat. Sister Martha smiled and nodded, and the woman nodded back. The man lifted his hat and murmured, "G'morning, Sister." As they moved past her, the woman said to Brooke, "Is that one of your teachers?" Brooke kept her eyes to the ground and didn't reply.

Sister Martha continued walking over to Gwen as the family made their way into the church, where people were converging from all directions. Approaching the fence with a sober expression, she said, "Hello, Gwen."

Gwen shifted from one foot to another.

"Are you all right, Gwen?"

"I'm okay," Gwen murmured.

"Is there something wrong? Can I help you?"

Gwen shook her head.

Sister Martha waited for her to speak, and when she remained silent, said, "Are you coming in to Mass? The school choir is singing."

"I don't know. Maybe."

"If you haven't been to Mass yet, you know you'll have to…"

"Just leave me alone, Sister." Her voice was barely audible.

Sister Martha turned away from the girl and walked to the church, her shoulders slumped. Inside, she climbed to the choir loft. Sister Estelle, who was lifting the leather cover from the organ, glared at her. At the back, three of the girls were giggling. One wore white shoes rather than the regulation black loafers. Sister Martha moved over to them. "Up to the front," she said in a whisper. The three continued to talk as if they hadn't heard her. "Up to the front, girls," she said aloud. She returned to Sister Estelle and whispered, indicating the choir girls, "We have to put up with this nonsense when there are girls who really need our help and our hands are tied because the Rule won't let us..."

Sister Estelle put her finger to her lips. When Mass began, Sister Martha scanned the congregation over the choir loft railing. Gwen was nowhere to be seen.

When all the people were inside and the church doors were closed, Gwen pulled away from the fence and walked in the opposite direction. She wandered the streets for the next few hours. She wore the same suede jacket and brown skirt from the day before. Her hair was tousled, and there was a wide run in one of her nylons. From time to time, she stopped to stare into store windows. At one store, winter coats with fur collars were already on display. The wind had picked up, and she pulled the collar of her jacket around her neck and thrust her hands into her pockets.

By the late afternoon she was standing on a street corner absently moving an empty Coke bottle about with her toe when a yellow convertible with the top up approached and slowed to a stop at the curb. J.J. rolled down the window. "Hey, Gwen, get in."

"Reverend Mother phoned and asked if I could pick up two of the nuns," she said after Gwen had settled into the seat beside her.

"How come she asked you?" Gwen's voice was flat.

"It's the price I have to pay for parking at the school. She never says who the nuns are or where we're going. It's all hush-hush. A mystery tour. Don't you remember picking up Sister Martha from the dentist?" She looked over at Gwen and grinned.

"Oh, yeah." Gwen gave a weak smile.

The day had become dismal. They drove past a park that was littered with orange and yellow leaves, the trees nearly bare, the playground empty. A light rain began to fall. "I picked you up just in time," J.J. said as she turned on the windshield wipers.

Gwen shivered. "I guess the nuns won't be too happy when they see me," she said.

"Well, that's tough," J.J. said. "They can take it or leave it. My dad wasn't too happy with them calling me on a Sunday, but I said I'd go, because she doesn't ask me too often."

As soon as the car pulled up to the curb outside the iron gate, the front door opened, and out stepped two nuns, their veils pulled forward to shield their faces.

"Get back there," J.J. said, pointing to the back seat. "Don't let them see your underwear." She grinned. "Remember, *Semper ubi sub ubi?*"

Gwen smiled again as she scrambled over into the back seat. When the nuns reached the car, they threw back their veils. Reverend Mother sat in the front, Sister Beatrice in the back. Gwen shrank into the corner. As the car began to move, Sister Beatrice reached forward and handed Reverend Mother a piece of paper with an address on it.

"It's the Hankey residence," Reverend Mother said to J.J. "Do you know where it is? You perhaps know Brooke Hankey?"

"I think so, Reverend Mother," J.J. said.

Gwen glanced over at Sister Beatrice, who looked straight ahead, moving her lips as if she was saying her prayers.

Gwen spoke up. "Is Sister Zélie okay?"

There was no response. J.J. came to a stop at a red light and turned to Reverend Mother. "Is Sister Zélie okay, Reverend Mother?"

"She's fine."

"When will she be coming back to school?" Gwen asked.

Reverend Mother made no response.

"Is she deaf?" Gwen asked Sister Beatrice. The nun shook her head in disapproval and continued looking straight ahead.

"When will she come back to school, Reverend Mother?" J.J. asked in a loud voice.

"When God wills it," Reverend Mother replied.

J.J. looked through the rear-view mirror at the shrunken figure of Gwen in one corner of the back seat. They drove on past modest bungalows, and turned onto a street where the houses became larger, some with three storeys, manicured gardens, and sweeping lawns. The afternoon sky had darkened, and lights were on in some of the windows. At the top of the hill stood a mansion with pillars in the front and a pathway that led to an enormous wooden front door. A chandelier glowed in one of the windows.

"Here we are," J.J. said.

"Mr. Hankey will drive us home," Reverend Mother said, and the two nuns got out and walked up the path to the front door.

After they had closed the car doors behind them, J.J. looked at Gwen in the rear-view mirror. "Get back up here. I'm not your chauffeur."

Gwen climbed back into the front seat.

They drove in silence as the rain became heavier. The wipers squeaked on the windshield.

"Brooke Hankey's father is rich," J.J. said finally. "She gets special treatment. That's why she got to sing for Reverend Mother's feast day rather than Sally. Did you see that page that someone put on the…"

"It's a mortal sin, isn't it?" Gwen broke in.

"What is?"

"Going all the way."

"At the last school retreat the priest said…"

"I know. He said that necking wasn't a mortal sin but that petting was. Then he didn't say anything more than that. As if he didn't think any of us would go any further."

"Actually, he said that necking was the 'near occasion of sin.' Isn't that how he put it? Anyway, what does it matter?"

"It matters a lot if it's a mortal sin and you're going to hell."

"But Gwen, the main thing is for you to have someone to talk to. And to make sure that it's what you think it is."

"If it is or isn't, it doesn't matter to God. I've committed a mortal sin."

"If you've committed a mortal sin, then so has the guy, hasn't he?"

"Well, sure, but that's his business. All he has to do is go to confession. Then he's scot-free. He doesn't have anything else to worry about."

As J.J. slowed the car for a red light, she said, "Is he from St. Paul's?"

"Let's say I get run over by a car, or we get into an accident right now and I'm killed. I'm going straight to hell."

J.J. started up the car again. "We can go to a priest right now, if you like. They have to hear your confession, no matter where they are or what they're doing, or whether they want to or not. St. Justin's is just ahead."

"Okay, take me there."

J.J. turned a corner and parked in front of the rectory beside St. Justin's Church. Together, the girls walked up to the door. J.J. rang the bell. The priest who answered the doorbell was middle-aged with a stomach that stretched the belt holding up his trousers. "Yes?" he said, then added, "Wait!" He looked back into the interior of the rectory, where a newscaster's voice could be heard on the television. The two girls looked at each other in silence. When he turned back to them, he said, "All right, they're saying the smoke's black. That means there's no new pope yet. What can I do for you?"

J.J. nudged Gwen, and when the other girl said nothing, she said, "Father, we'd like to go to confession."

"We hear confessions before the morning Masses. Why didn't you go then?"

"We weren't here then." J.J. looked at Gwen.

Gwen then spoke in a subdued voice. "We'll just take a minute, Father."

"Very well." He gestured to the church.

Inside, the incense from the earlier High Mass still lingered in the air. The light from the votive candles in front of the side altars cast shadows over the sanctuary. J.J. knelt at a far pew and stared at the sanctuary lamp and the white-curtained tab-ernacle. The priest appeared from a side entrance and gestured to one of the confessionals.

Inside the dark curtained space, Gwen knelt on the wooden kneeler and faced the screen on which the priest's dim silhouette could be seen. She began in a whisper: "Bless me Father, for I have sinned. I didn't go to Mass today."

"And why not?"

"I didn't feel like it."

"Didn't *feel* like it? Holy Mass has nothing to do with your feelings. Tell God you're sorry, and that you'll do your best to attend Mass on Sundays from now on. That's a good girl now. Just say your act of contrition."

"That's not all, Father. I went all the way."

"All the way with what?"

"With someone. A guy."

"Do you mean you committed a sin against the sixth com-mandment?"

"Yes, Father."

"Well now, that is serious. Is this your first time?"

"Yes, Father."

"So it is still possible for you to amend your life. How old are you?"

"Sixteen, Father."

"Sixteen. Such a young age. Girls like yourself excite the opposite sex, lead them into temptation. You cause them to sin by the way you dress, the way you behave. Is this not true?"

Gwen didn't answer.

"Is this not true?" he said again.

"I guess so."

"You *guess* so? I *know* so. But almighty God will forgive that sin, and your soul will be pure again. In one of the psalms it says, 'Wash me, and I will be made whiter than snow.' That's what you're asking for now, isn't? For your soul to be made whiter than snow?"

"Yes, Father."

"You must also resolve to dress modestly. No part of your breasts must show. Breasts are a great temptation to the opposite sex. And your dresses must not be revealing. Boys are always tempted by a girl's legs. It's a terrible thing to be the occasion of another person's sin."

"Yes, Father." Gwen buttoned the top of her blouse.

"So now, say your act of contrition. When you have a contrite heart, God forgives all your sins."

"Father, what if I'm ... what if I'm ... let's say, going to have a baby. And let's say it ... let's say it dies before it's born. For some reason."

The priest was silent for a long moment. "Are you going to have a baby?"

"I don't know. Maybe."

"And are you thinking of the unthinkable? Of killing it? Of murder?"

"I'm just wondering. If it dies for some reason, will its soul go to heaven?"

"Without baptism, the soul of an innocent child goes to limbo."

"It can't go to heaven?"

"You must tell me that if you are going to have a baby, you will not kill it."

There was silence.

"Tell me that, or you won't receive absolution. Your soul will remain in the state of mortal sin."

"Yes, Father."

"Yes what?"

"Yes, I won't kill it. But I don't even know..."

"You must be sorry for even thinking you might do it."

"But Father, I don't know if I thought it or not. It's just that I wouldn't want any soul not to go to heaven. Not even the soul of a baby."

"Just tell me you are sorry for all your sins, those you have committed, and those you have thought about committing."

"I'm sorry, Father."

"For all your sinful thoughts, words, and deeds?"

"Yes, Father."

"Then I absolve you. Say a decade of the rosary for your penance. What school do you go to?"

Gwen hesitated, and her voice, when she spoke, was barely audible. "St. Monica's."

"They're good sisters. They'll help you out. God bless you now."

Outside the confessional, Gwen knelt briefly, counting the Hail Marys on her fingers. Back in the car, her eyes were expressionless as she examined her bitten fingernails.

"Feel better?" J.J. said.

"I guess so. I still don't know what to do. He said the nuns would help me. Yeah, sure. Sister Beatrice wouldn't even talk to me in the car. Fat lot of help she's going to be."

"Sister Beatrice probably had other things on her mind. She and Reverend Mother weren't going to Brooke Hankey's house just to have tea and crumpets. The nuns don't go into people's homes. Not without some important reason, anyway."

Gwen said nothing. J.J. went on, "Sister Zélie may still answer your letter. Even if she doesn't, she won't stay away from school forever. We hope so, anyway."

"I saw Sister Martha outside Purification Church this morning. She asked me if something was wrong."

"What did you tell her?"

"I didn't tell her anything."

"If she asked whether something was wrong, it means that at least she cares about you. Maybe that's all the nuns can do."

"Yeah." Gwen settled in her seat and looked out at the rain. The car splashed through puddles on its way back to the centre of the city.

"But you have friends. You've got me."

Gwen gave a weak smile.

"To Betty's for a hamburger and milkshake?" J.J. said. Gwen nodded. "Sure."

12. Holy Rule

THE WOMAN SCANNED THE GREY STONE of the convent wall as she pressed the doorbell. She was short, with grey hair, dark eyebrows, and worry lines in her forehead. She wore a rather shabby green coat.

Sister Antonetta appeared at the door. "Yes," she said without inflection.

"Sister, may I see Reverend Mother, please?"

Sister Antonetta peered at her.

"It *is* important."

The old nun said, "Come in," without enthusiasm.

The woman stepped inside.

"Does Reverend Mother know you're coming?" Sister Antonetta asked.

"I'm afraid not. I've just come from the hospital, you see, and I wasn't able to phone her. I'm Sister Zélie's mother."

"Sister Zélie? Is she...?"

"She's fine, I'm sure. But you would know that better than I. I haven't seen her since the summer, of course. It's her brother I've come to ask about."

"Her brother?"

"Yes. He's in St. Luke's Hospital. I'd like to ask Reverend Mother's permission..."

"You don't know...?" Sister Antonetta fluttered her arms and looked around the vestibule. "Just wait here. No...." She ushered the woman to the parlour door. "Wait in there."

In the parlour, the spikes of a large green plant stood sharply against the light coming in through the window. The woman sat on the edge of the sofa and placed her black purse beside her. After a few minutes, the rustle of rosary beads announced a nun's approach, and immediately Reverend Mother's large bulk appeared in the parlour doorway.

The woman stood up. "Reverend Mother, I'm sorry to bother you, but you see, I'm frantic with worry over my son, Tom. I can hardly think straight. They gave him transfusions and we thought he would..." She began to weep and rifled through her purse for a tissue.

"Sit down, Mrs. Aubin." Reverend Mother's voice was unusually gentle. The woman sat back down on the sofa, and the nun settled on a straight-backed chair and arranged her black skirt over her lap. She placed her elbows on the arms of the chair.

Mrs. Aubin wiped her eyes. "He has leukemia. He's only been in the hospital for a week, but it looks as if there's nothing more that can be done for him. And so, Reverend Mother, he's asking for his sister. I know that Sister Zélie gave up all possibility of ever visiting her family again when she entered the convent, but if you could find it in your heart to give her permission to visit him, it would mean so much."

Reverend Mother opened and closed her big hands. "I know this is a heartache for you, Mrs. Aubin, and I'll have the nuns pray for Tom, but we must leave him in God's hands. We do have a Rule, and that Rule must be obeyed."

"Yes, I know that, Reverend Mother, but Tom is crying out for his sister..."

"Our Rule allows us to have our families visit us here in the convent three times a year, as you know. That's a consolation, as I'm sure you agree."

"But I'm asking for just this one exception to the rule." She clutched her purse and moved to the edge of the sofa. "When our daughter entered the convent, she might as well have died to us. Her father has never gotten over it. Now, our son is dying too."

Reverend Mother smiled thinly. "That's the nature of sacrifice, Mrs. Aubin. We give ourselves over completely, without reserve. I couldn't ask anything less from Sister Zélie."

"You mean..."

"You will see that God rewards sacrifices such as this. God will bless Sister Zélie and will bless you abundantly because of it. And God will bless Tom as he prepares to enter eternity. There is a period in purgatory, of course, as there is for all of us, but let's say a prayer together. For him and for Sister Zélie."

Sister Zélie's eyes were half-closed when a plump new nurse entered her hospital room. Everything in the room was white: the bed frame, the coverings, and the curtains.

"Am I in heaven?" Sister Zélie said in a hoarse voice. "I must have been dozing."

The nurse laughed as she helped the nun raise herself against the propped-up pillows. Sister Zélie's nightcap fell open, the strings dangling on either side of her neck, her cropped head exposed. The nurse tied the two string ends together under her chin.

"Do you teach at St. Monica's?" she asked as she popped a thermometer into Sister Zélie's mouth. The thermometer, poking out, bobbed up and down as she nodded.

"I went to St. Monica's," the nurse continued. She held onto Sister Zélie's pulse and looked at her wristwatch. "It was more than ten years ago. I don't remember you. Were you teaching there in the forties?"

Sister Zélie shook her head, the thermometer moving now from side to side.

"We made fun of some of the nuns. We were actually mean sometimes. I remember sticking out my tongue at one of them. She was an old nun and could hardly walk, and yet she was still teaching school!" She looked at Sister Zélie, who made no visible reaction. "We used to wonder what the nuns' names really were. And we liked to imagine what they looked like underneath their habits. And here you are! Your hair is like a boy's, but you're a normal person!" She pulled the thermometer out of Sister Zélie's mouth and recorded the temperature on her chart. "Temp is normal too," she said, smiling. She adjusted the bedcovers with a plump pink arm.

Sister Zélie smiled and sank back onto the pillow.

"By the way, Sister, there's another patient upstairs with the same last name as yours. Aubin. It's not a well-known name around here." She leaned against the edge of the bed, as if she were going to sit down "I thought, isn't that an interesting coincidence, having two names the same on two different floors. Do you think you might be related?"

Sister Zélie raised her dark eyebrows. "I shouldn't be speaking to you. We have a rule about keeping silence." She smiled with a worried frown that gave the appearance of a grimace. "But there's no rule about you speaking to me. What's the other person's name?"

"I shouldn't have told you," the nurse said. "So we've both done something we shouldn't have. Anyway, I forget."

She returned a few moments later. "Tom," she said. "Tom Aubin."

Sister Zélie went white. "Tom?" she whispered.

The nurse nodded.

"What's wrong with him, did they say?"

The nurse's face had become grave. She shook her head.

Sister Zélie turned her face to the curtain. She said no more.

Sometime later, she opened her eyes to see Dr. Sullivan standing at the foot of the bed. He wore a white lab coat and held a pen and a clipboard. He looked at her over his brown-rimmed glasses when she began to move. "How are you this...?"

"Is it true?" Sister Zélie blurted out. "Is Tom a patient here?"

"I don't know. Who's Tom?"

"Tom's my twin brother. Is it true he's here in the hospital?"

"I don't know. I'd have to check." He looked at his clipboard. "If he was a patient here, wouldn't you know about it?"

"Only if Reverend Mother saw fit to tell me. And she's..." She paused, then continued: "I'm sorry, Doctor, I didn't mean to say it that way."

"Ye-es. Reverend Mother," he said slowly. He added something under his breath, then went on: "I'll check it out and let you know." He turned to leave and then approached the bed again. "Doesn't your family know you're here?"

"I don't know. I don't think so. Nobody's been here to see me, except for Reverend Mother and Sister Virginia, the infirmarian."

"I see. Well, I'll find out if that's your brother, and if he is, I'll have you wheeled to his room." As he walked out of the room, he muttered, "I've had enough of that woman."

A spot of colour appeared on Sister Zélie's pale face and she struggled to tie the strings of her nightcap as a burly hospital worker placed his arms around her and gently moved her onto the wheelchair. She wore a plain black dressing gown over her nightdress. Dr. Sullivan stood by, grim-faced. The hospital corridor was filled with the sound of nurses' chatter and the bustle of gurneys and the clean smell of disinfectant. They wheeled her past carts containing sheets and towels and workers wielding mops and brooms. Then, they wheeled her onto an empty elevator. Upstairs, inside a patient's room, Mrs. Aubin stood beside the bed. Her purse dangled from her hand. She turned with surprise as Sister Zélie was wheeled into the room.

"You didn't know I was here, Mama?" Sister Zélie said.

The figure on the bed turned his head, his thin face similar to his sister's. His pallor was almost blue.

"Sis, is that you? I knew you'd come."

Mrs. Aubin stared at her daughter. "What are you doing here? What is wrong with you? Reverend Mother said nothing...."

"I had an operation, Mama. That's all." She leaned over the bed. "Hi there, Tom."

"Why didn't Reverend Mother say something?"

"When did you speak to Reverend Mother, Mama?"

"Just this morning. I asked if you could get permission to see Tom because he was asking for you. Reverend Mother said…" She stopped, raised her hand to her face, and whispered, "She said no."

Sister Zélie sat forward. "She said no? She didn't tell you that I was here?"

Her mother shook her head. She dabbed her eyes with a tissue. "She said it was a sacrifice that would please God."

Sister Zélie looked over at Tom. "I'm glad that nurse told me…."

Her mother pushed the wheelchair until she was now flush with the hospital bed. "I'm not going to make it, Sis." There was a thin smile on his face.

Sister Zélie winced as she adjusted her position in the chair. "Sure you will, Tom," she said. "We're all praying for you." She turned to her mother. "I'm going back to the convent later today. So it was lucky I was able to get here."

Her mother's eyes filled with tears. She said nothing.

"I didn't even know Tom was sick," Sister Zélie said.

"I wrote you a letter last week. I was going to phone, but I didn't think you'd be allowed to take a phone call."

"That's right. Also, you must remember that we receive letters only once a month, on the first Sunday."

"Zélie, what kind of an operation did you have? And why didn't Reverend Mother tell me this morning?"

"She didn't tell you because…" Sister Zélie fell silent. She looked at the emaciated figure of her brother. "I guess she didn't want you to worry about me. You're worried enough as it is."

"She could at least have said you had an operation and are getting better. You *are* getting better, aren't you, Zélie?"

"Oh yes, the operation was successful."

"What was it? Did you have your appendix out?"

Sister Zélie put her hand to the side of her midriff.

"No, it was more complicated than that. It was a rupture in the uterus."

Mrs. Aubin put her hand to her mouth and gasped. "But that's serious! You could have died!"

"Yes," Sister Zélie said quietly. "I could have. That's what Doctor Sullivan said."

"Then why didn't the nuns tell me?"

"It's not 'the nuns,' Mama. It's Reverend Mother. The other nuns have nothing to do with it. They may not even know I'm in the hospital. Though some of them have a way of nosing things out—they know, but the others don't. Reverend Mother probably asked their prayers for 'one of ours who is sick' or something vague like that. 'Someone who has had a serious operation.' They'll be able to put two and two together, but my name will never be mentioned."

"But who's looking after your classes?"

"Sister Beatrice is filling in for me. Or one of the old retired nuns. Maybe they'll combine one of my classes with another one in the auditorium. They do that sometimes when one of the nuns is sick. The girls will be curious, of course. I collapsed in the class...."

"You what? You collapsed where?"

"Never mind, Mama. It doesn't matter. Reverend Mother knows best. She's been very good to me. I shouldn't have told you anything about this."

Tom stirred on the bed and turned his head toward the two women. "Thanks for coming, Sis."

"I'm sorry," Reverend Mother said in her usual deep, mannish voice. She held her rosary in her large hand and fingered a bead. "Your mother telephoned this morning. Your brother died during the night."

She stood at the foot of the bed, her big-boned figure a looming presence in the convent's small infirmary room. Her face had settled into deep furrows of wrinkles. "Your mother said he had a very peaceful death."

Sister Zélie leaned back against two propped-up pillows. Two strings at the neck of her white nightgown dangled in front of her chest. Her nightcap was fastened underneath her chin. On her lap sat a breakfast tray covered with a linen cloth. A plate with a domed lid had not been touched, and a piece of toast that had been broken into four pieces remained uneaten. She withdrew her hands from beneath the bedclothes and threw her thin white arms, which were lined with sharply defined blue veins, on either side of the tray. She looked straight ahead without speaking.

The infirmary room had a high ceiling, but the dark, ornate furniture gave the impression of oppressiveness. Against one wall stood an imposing mahogany wardrobe and chest of drawers, and against the other, an elaborate washstand. A bay window allowed the morning sunlight to break in upon the heaviness.

"She's taking it very well," Reverend Mother said into the silence of the room. "There's much consolation in the last rites. No one could have been better prepared for death."

Sister Zélie remained motionless, staring into space. Reverend Mother walked around the bed to the washstand, picked up a towel that hung along the side, refolded it, and placed it back. She faced Sister Zélie again, fingering the large rosary at her side. "There will be ten Masses said for the repose of his soul, of course." When the other nun still hadn't responded, she added in an unusually quiet and gentle voice, "May he rest in peace."

As she turned to leave, Sister Zélie slid the tray to the side of the bed, wincing. Coffee spilled onto the saucer. Still staring ahead, she said, "He's my twin."

Reverend Mother turned back. "We must accept God's holy

will, Sister." Throwing her veil over her shoulder, she picked up the tray. "Try to rest quietly."

A knock came to the door and the infirmarian, Sister Virginia, appeared. "Oh, Mother, excuse me, I didn't realize," she said, backing out of the doorway.

"Come in, come in, come in," Reverend Mother said, frowning.

Her face flushed, Sister Virginia entered the room. She reached out for the tray. "Let me, Mother," she said, bowing as Reverend Mother handed it to her. Reverend Mother turned to leave.

"My mother didn't say that," Sister Zélie called after her. Reverend Mother turned back, her mouth open.

"My mother didn't say, 'He had a peaceful death.' She doesn't talk like that. You made it up."

Sister Virginia stood rigid, her cheeks flaming.

"You must rest now, Sister. You're tired," Reverend Mother said. She left the room and the infirmarian closed the door behind her.

"Do you realize what you just said?" Sister Virginia held the tray in a tight grip.

"You didn't even address her as 'Mother'! How could you?"

"Well, she did make it up. She…" Sister Zélie's face contorted and then crumpled.

Sister Virginia rushed to the side of the bed. "Lie down now and get some rest. Try to sleep." She arranged the pillow as Sister Zélie slid down between the sheets. "That was a serious operation, you know. You have to be quiet and rest or else you'll be right back the way you were before." She tiptoed backwards. "May he rest in peace," she whispered.

In the corridor outside her office, Reverend Mother waited as Sister Antonetta hurried over to her with the newspaper folded on a silver tray. She took the newspaper from the tray, opened it to the front page, and fumbled in her pocket for her reading glasses. The top headline read, in thick letters,

"RONCALLI," Sister Antonetta bowed and opened the office door for her, then stepped aside as Reverend Mother entered, and closed it quietly.

A soft knock sounded at the door and it opened tentatively. Sister Clementia poked her head in the doorway, the ends of her veil tied back behind her shoulders. "Excuse me, Mother, shall I run the dust mop over the floor?"

"Come in, Sister." Reverend Mother glanced up briefly.

Sister Clementia padded inside and proceeded to mop the floor with short, quick movements.

"We have a new Holy Father," Reverend Mother said, her eyes still on the newspaper.

Sister Clementia stopped and looked up. "Oh, very good, Mother, very good." She waited, and when Reverend Mother said no more, she resumed mopping the floor.

"He's going to be Pope John the..." Reverend Mother stopped for a second, her lips moving silently. "...The twenty-third." She looked toward the window. "It says here, he combines the skill of a diplomat with the skill of a pastor of souls. That's the secular world for you. Nothing about the work of the Holy Ghost." She looked down at the newspaper again. "It says here, 'Elected on the eleventh ballot.' You'd think it was a political election."

"God bless him, Mother," Sister Clementia said. She turned to the bookcase and ran a feather duster along the top shelf.

"He's been the patriarch of Venice. A cardinal, of course. Do you know why the patriarch of Venice is called a patriarch?"

Sister Clementia began to back up toward the door. "No, Mother."

"In ages gone by, patriarchs had a great deal of worldly power and authority. Now, of course, their power is all in the supernatural realm, which is as it should be."

"Is that so, Mother."

"Here he is." Reverend Mother held out the newspaper's front page. The picture showed a rotund man in white, his face half hidden in shadows, his right hand raised in blessing. A priest stood to one side of him, holding a large book, from which the new pope appeared to be reading "He's seventy-six years old," Reverend Mother said. "Far different in appearance from our last Holy Father,"

"Isn't he lovely, Mother," Sister Clementia said. She opened the door, still facing into the room. "Excuse me, Mother." She backed out and closed the door.

Sister Clementia hurried down the corridor to the back staircase and made her way to the basement. In the kitchen, a white-veiled novice was peeling potatoes, another was sifting flour into a large bowl. Sister Kate stood at the stove, emptying the contents of a huge can into a pot. The three were reciting the rosary together as they worked. Sister Clementia tiptoed out and headed to the laundry.

There, Lizzie was pushing sheets through a steam press. Sister Clementia spoke in a whisper. "There's a new Holy Father, Lizzie." She ran her hands under the hot water tap in the big sink.

Lizzie looked up. "Thanks be to God, Sister. I thought we were never going to get a new pope."

"It took eleven ballots. That's what Reverend Mother said."

"And who is he then, Sister?"

"He's short and round." Sister Clementia made a wide circle with her arms in front of her. "Pope John, he's to be called."

"Pope John. Fancy that. God bless him." Lizzie made the sign of the cross and resumed guiding the sheets through the press.

"A patriarch, Lizzie. That's what he is."

"The good man. May God guide him for many years to come."

"He's old, Lizzie. In his seventies. He doesn't have many years ahead of him."

"I suppose not. But please God he'll keep the Russians from coming here and boiling us all in oil. That's what they do to Catholics, you know, Sister."

"We should say the rosary now, Lizzie, for the new Holy

Father." Sister Clementia plunged her hands into a tub where white underclothes had been set to soak.

At noon, the Angelus bell from Purification Church began to ring. Reverend Mother emerged from her office and walked to the chapel. From various parts of the convent, other nuns did the same. Then the novices began to arrive, one by one, until they knelt, twelve of them, white-veiled, four to a pew. The red sanctuary lamp, glowing inside its gold casing, hung in the centre of the sanctuary. The chapel was quiet, and as the pealing of the Angelus bells continued, a flurry of nuns arrived, breathless, from St. Monica's. Reverend Mother knelt and began the Angelus: "The angel of the Lord declared unto Mary…"

When the prayer ended, she got up, genuflected, and left the chapel. Downstairs, she paused at the refectory door and continued on to the kitchen. Sister Kate froze at the sight of her and gave a stiff bow. Sister Virginia, who was preparing a tray, stopped, holding a clutch of cutlery in mid-air, and bowed.

"I'll take up Sister Zélie's tray." Reverend Mother brushed the infirmarian aside and picked up the tray. It had been set with an embroidered cutwork runner. She picked up the cloth. "This is a piece I embroidered."

The two nuns stayed frozen in place, watching her. She continued fingering it and appeared lost in thought.

"A million years ago, that was. The edging has held up well all this time." She returned the cloth to the tray and gestured to Sister Kate. "Some soup here," she said.

Sister Kate sprang back into movement. She ladled some soup into a bowl and placed it on the tray. "Bread and butter," she said. "Some lettuce. A dish of fruit. That's all, I think, Mother."

"Are you not giving her a slice of meat? She needs it to recover her strength."

"Oh, yes, Mother." Sister Kate ran to the walk-in refrigerator and emerged holding a plate of roast beef. She sliced off two pieces and put them on the plate.

"And a top to keep the soup warm," Reverend Mother said.

"Yes, Mother, here," Sister Virginia said from behind, holding a domed top.

Reverend Mother felt the small teapot for warmth and inspected the tray. "A glass of milk," she said finally. Again, the cook sprang over to the refrigerator and emerged with a gallon jug of milk.

Sister Virginia followed Reverend Mother to the base of the stairs. "Mother, are you sure you wouldn't like me to carry it up?"

Without answering, Reverend Mother positioned the tray in one hand and fumbled with the other to hold up her skirt. She proceeded up the stairs.

"Oh, please watch yourself, Mother," Sister Virginia called after her.

The infirmarian returned to the kitchen. "I don't know why she's paying so much attention to Sister Zélie," she whispered. "You should have heard how that little upstart spoke to her."

"Ah well, poor Zélie's just lost her brother, God rest his soul," Sister Kate whispered back, then put her finger to her lips.

Sister Zélie lay motionless on her back and watched as Reverend Mother approached the bed with awkward steps. The tray in her hands listed to one side. The silver top had slid off and a puddle of soup flooded the rim of the plate underneath. Breathing hard, she set the tray down at Sister Zélie's feet.

"We'll have to get you sitting up."

Sister Zélie inched herself up as Reverend Mother arranged the pillow upright behind her. The superior then picked up the tray and placed it on the invalid nun's lap. "A nice bowl of soup and some cold roast beef."

Sister Zélie's hands remained at her side.

Reverend Mother drew the chair from the corner to the bedside and sat, arranging the folds of her habit skirt. "We have a new Holy Father," she said.

Sister Zélie gave a quiet sigh. She regarded the tray with its pool of spilled soup around the bowl and looked over at Reverend Mother, a hint of insolence in her dark eyes.

"He's going to be known as Pope John the twenty-third. It will take some getting used to." Reverend Mother gave a slight smile. "He's as roly-poly as our saintly late Holy Father was thin and ascetic. But the cardinals know what they're doing. It's the Holy Ghost's work."

Sister Zélie took the white cloth napkin from the tray and spread it over her chest. She picked up the spoon in a slow, even movement, and sifted through the soup. Rice, peas and small pieces of carrots and onions rose to the surface. She grimaced. "Onions. I hate onions."

"A nice bit of mortification for you." Reverend Mother's face softened.

Sister Zélie put her spoon down.

"You were close to your brother, Sister. Twins are always close."

The invalid dropped her hands to her side.

"He was prepared for death, and that's a consolation. The last rites of the Church are the best send-off anyone can wish for."

Sister Zélie poured tea into her cup.

"Drink the milk too. You need your strength."

Sister Zélie sipped her tea. Reverend Mother got up and walked over to the bay window. Outside, the sky was blue and cloudless. The copper steeple of Purification Church shone in the sunshine. "I remember when the news came of my brother Jack's death," she said, turning back. "He was killed in Belgium. 1915. The Great War, as we called it. I can still see my father pounding his feet on the floor of the porch and coming in and sitting down at the kitchen table. He looked at my mother and said, 'Something's happened to Jack. I can feel it.' He spread his big rough hand over his chest. Sure enough, the telegram came. And just two or three winters before, it was my youngest brother Micky. He died of typhoid just like that..." She snapped her fingers and walked back to the bed. "He was just a little fellow, thirteen years old. The ground was too frozen to bury him, so he had to be kept in his coffin in one of the sheds until the spring. It was all dreadfully hard on my poor mother."

Sister Zélie stared at her without speaking.

"We're told to give up our families when we enter religious life," Reverend Mother went on as she returned to her chair, "but it isn't as easy as all that. If it was, it wouldn't be a sacrifice. Still, it's a great burden on our families. Especially in Orders like ours where we do not ever return to our families. It's a sacrifice that of course we offer joyfully to God, but for our families..." She shook her head.

Sister Zélie slid down the bed until the tray was on top of her chest and her napkin covered her chin. She continued to stare at Reverend Mother.

"I remember when I left home to enter the novitiate," Reverend Mother went on. "I was a late vocation, already in my early thirties and teaching school, but still living at home. On my way to becoming a selfish old maid. There were just the two of us left then, Gerald and myself, Jack and Micky having died, and my mother was proud that I was giving my life to God, but I could tell she was also heartbroken. Gerald tried to make light of it, going around the house singing, '*Toot, toot, Tootsie, goodbye.*' But my leaving was very hard on everybody just the same."

Sister Zélie slid onto her elbows. "What did he sing?"

"It was a popular song of the day." Reverend Mother stopped in thought, then striking the beat with her hand, sang in a cracked half-whisper, "*Toot, toot, Tootsie, goodbye. Toot, toot, Tootsie, don't cry.*" She smiled. "Then, of course, I left home for the novitiate, never to return." She folded and unfolded her hands. "Gerald took the farm over when my father became too ill to carry on. And now, he's gone as well. That's my whole family."

She reached over to the tray, which now tilted to one side of the bed. More soup had spilled over, staining the runner underneath and soaking the bread. She lifted the glass of milk, which stood almost ready to spill over as well, and held it to Sister Zélie.

Sister Zélie shook her head. Her face contorted with pain as she tried to sit up.

"I remember the noise and grime of the train station when I left," Reverend Mother went on. "The steam engine puffing away and the men calling out, and then the polished, silent corridor of the convent." She smiled. "The pang when I took off my hat for the last time. It was a red felt hat, with a tall feather, and I thought myself very grand wearing it. I was a vain young woman."

Sister Zélie worked her way into a half-sitting position.

"And did I get my comeuppance! Confined in a small space, seeing the same people day after day, the strict rule of silence. This may surprise you, but I enjoyed the company of men. After all, I was the only girl with three brothers. I found having only women for company a very difficult penance. But that's what we're here for, isn't it? To do penance. To make reparation for the sins of others. To become saints."

"When did Gerald die?"

Reverend Mother looked sharply at Sister Zélie. "Why do you ask that? Nearly thirty years ago. A farm accident." Her eyes grew moist. "He had taken himself a witch of a wife. That's what my mother called her—'Gerald's witch.' Once that woman was installed in the house, my mother no longer had the run of things. She always held that the witch didn't mend his clothes properly, and that's why his jacket got entangled in the machinery." She took a breath. "After the accident, my poor mother was cast out even further. She'd buried her husband and three sons. Her only daughter, who could have been a help and a consolation to her, was shut up in the cloister."

Sister Zélie smoothed the sheet. She reached for the glass of milk and took a sip.

Reverend Mother drew a large white handkerchief from her pocket and dabbed her eyes. "In some ways, religious life is not very Christ-like. It can seem cruel. But the Church has entrusted me with the duty and responsibility of upholding the Holy Rule, and I do it to the best of my ability. The idea behind our Rule, of course, is that we give our all to God, that we forsake everything to follow Him." Her voice rose. "It is required of me to make sure the Holy Rule is kept to the letter, and that I will do with all my might and all my strength. I am nothing if not obedient to the Church." She sat up straight.

Sister Zélie finished drinking the milk and returned the glass to the tray. She pushed the tray away from her.

"Penance is not our life's purpose, Sister." Reverend Mother replaced her handkerchief in her pocket. "Our purpose is to lose ourselves completely so that God might live in us. We do not deliberately inflict hardship on anyone." She looked directly at Sister Zélie, as if expecting her to speak, but the younger nun remained silent.

"You have no idea how it is to have the responsibility of a religious superior." Reverend Mother shook her head vigorously, twisting and untwisting her hands. "No idea of what it takes to tell someone a family member has died, or that their vocation is in danger because they are failing in silence and obedience. Or..." She turned to the door, as if to make sure it was closed. "Or what it takes to get the wherewithal for a school like St. Monica's to run as it should. The decisions you have to make, sometimes to the detriment of what you think is right..." Her voice broke off and she stared down at her hands.

"You could ask to be relieved of the responsibility if you're not up to it."

"Relieved? *Relieved*? Is this what we're doing in religious life? Is this why we left all to follow Our Lord's call—to be *relieved*? Is this what you've learned? How many years has it been for you?"Sister Zélie leaned back onto the pillow. A defiant look fell over her face. "I've got news for you Mother. I know what happened."

Reverend Mother went still, a frown on her face.

"Yesterday morning, my mother asked you if I could have permission to see Tom. He was in another wing. You told her no. You said, 'This isn't our way.' You said something about the grace this sacrifice would bring. But guess what? Doctor Sullivan had them wheel me down to see Tom. Poor Tom—he looked so thin and in so much pain that I could hardly stand it."

Reverend Mother's eyes narrowed.

"Do you want to hear more, Mother? Doctor Sullivan told me that an abscess like I had could have killed me. And you told me to put up with the pain for the love of God. Until the day I collapsed."

The wrinkles in Reverend Mother's face seemed to harden like wax. "A superior's judgment is only human. God knows I face the tabernacle every day with the knowledge of my many failings. But you must realize the only way for a nun to know the will of God is to submit her own will in holy obedience. Think of those saints who became holy because of their superiors' failings. Saints like Saint Bernadette. And you look at me with your hard eyes and profess disobedience—I think, Sister, you are not on the path of the saints."

Sister Zélie's hands were limp at her side. "Was it my fault that the doctor ordered me to be wheeled to Tom's room? Was it my fault that he said, 'I've had enough of that woman'? It took me a minute to realize that he was referring to you."

Reverend Mother sat as stiff as stone, her lips a straight line, her hands gripped together in her lap. She looked above the bed at the black crucifix and back at Sister Zélie. "We are called to forsake all, to become saints, and the most sure way is through the vow of obedience." Her voice was a low drone. "To bend my will to the will of God. The superior is the mouthpiece of God. If she makes life miserable for everyone, then she alone must answer to God for it." She pointed a large finger at Sister Zélie. "But those under her authority advance in sanctity through obedience."

"I wish I could believe that, Mother. Doctor Sullivan said, 'You teach French at St. Monica's, one of the most respected schools in the city, and you let that woman dictate to you about your health?'"

Reverend Mother waved her hand dismissively. "He sees things as the world does, not the way a religious does. He has no idea of what it means to follow Jesus, who became obedient unto death." She stood up. "Now you must rest. I want to be able to tell your mother that you're recovering well."

Lizzie came into the laundry by the outside door, as she always did. "It's because of the change, the doctor says. That's what he calls it. The change."

Sister Clementia was pushing clothes through the wringer. "What change, Lizzie?"

"The change of life, Sister!"

"What's because of the change of life?"

"Me headaches!" Lizzie put her hand in the huge washing machine and pulled out an undershirt. "Oh, Sister, I'm sorry," she said, returning it to the machine. "I thought they were tea towels and pillowcases in there."

"A silly rule, Lizzie, that you can't touch the nuns' things."

"But rules is rules, Sister. A nun is specially consecrated, and her clothes is consecrated too. Who knows, but one day we may be venerating a piece of one of your undershirts as a relic. Saint Clementia!"

Sister Clementia's face broke into a wide grin and she passed a hand over her perspiring brow. "No, Lizzie, there'll be too much mending on them, for one thing. And for another, I'm not a saint. Not quite." She chuckled.

"Sister, was that two of your nuns I saw when I was passing by St. Joseph's Church yesterday?"

"Couldn't have been, Lizzie. We don't go anywhere, except to the doctor. It's in our Rule somewhere."

"There was a funeral. I stopped while they took the casket in, as I always do, and I said a Hail Mary for the repose of the soul of the poor departed, and then after everyone was inside, the family and that, I saw two nuns get out of a car and go in a side door."

"We don't go to funerals. Except our own, of course, here in our chapel."

"I could have sworn it was your Reverend Mother. And one of the younger ones. I don't know her name. They were sort of hanging on to each other."

"Sister Zélie lost her brother a few days ago, may he rest in peace. But no. Reverend Mother would never allow it. She's very strict about these things." Sister Clementia dried her hands and made for the door. "I'll check the sheets on the line outside."

"Well, if she did allow it, I say God bless her," Lizzie called after her.

Sister Clementia returned with an armful of sheets. "These can be pressed now, Lizzie."

Acknowledgements

A big debt of gratitude to Alissa York and the Wired Writing Program at the Banff Centre for Arts and Creativity. Thanks to the Ontario Arts Council for a Work-in-Progress Grant. And many thanks as well to Barry Webster for reading parts of the manuscript, and to Luciana Ricciutelli and Renée Knapp of Inanna Publications.

Mary Frances Coady was born in Saskatchewan and raised in Alberta. She now lives in Toronto. She is the author of a collection of linked short stories, *The Practice of Perfection*, as well as of several biographies and young adult fiction. Her work has also appeared in *The Antigonish Review, The Dalhousie Review, The Fiddlehead, Whetstone, Commonweal*, and other publications. She has taught at Centennial College and Sheridan College, and has also worked as an editor and creative writing instructor. She currently teaches professional communication at Ryerson University in Toronto.